Summer Fling

Compass Girls, book 3

Mari Carr & Jayne Rylon

Copyright 2017 by Mari Carr

All Rights Reserved.

No part of this book, with the exception of brief quotations for book reviews or critical articles, may be reproduced or transmitted in any form or by any means, electronic or mechanical, including photocopying, recording, or by any information storage and retrieval system without express written permission from the author.

This is a work of fiction. Names, characters, places, and incidents are the product of the author's imagination or are used fictitiously, and any resemblance to actual persons, living or dead, business establishments, events, or locales is entirely coincidental.

ISBN: 978-1544792989

Editor: Amy Sherwood

Cover artist: Jayne Rylon

Print formatting: Mari Carr

Summertime and the lovin' is easy...until it's not.

Too much love and loss taught Jade Compton to protect her heart and her sanity by steering clear of all that romance nonsense. She's doing just fine, working two jobs, hanging out with her cousins and her best friend, Liam.

But when a combination of unbearable heat wave and a case of the boredom blues knocks her down, she longs to do something spontaneous...maybe even a little bit reckless.

Liam Harrison met Jade when she was sixteen—in the local cemetery. If he's learned anything after eight years of friendship, it's that Jade has a wild streak a mile wide. And while he doesn't want to tame the adventurous woman, he wouldn't mind showing her a few sexy ways to channel some of her impulsiveness. With him. In the bedroom.

When he proposes a sexy, no-strings-attached summer fling, Jade jumps at the chance to spice things up and indulge some pretty kinky fantasies. Then summer ends...and Jade comes to the uncomfortable realization that there's only one place she's comfortable in her own skin—Liam's arms.

Dedication

To our very first heroes, our dads, Roger and Glenn. They taught us the true meaning of strength, commitment and unconditional love.

Prologue

Jade Compton pulled her scarf tighter around her neck and ignored the biting cold as she picked her way slowly through the cemetery. Streetlamps illuminated her trip to the church, but the lack of moonlight—thanks to a cloudy sky—became apparent the second she stepped off the sidewalk and into the graveyard.

She was a fool for making this pilgrimage alone in the middle of the night, but the need to come here had tugged at her consciousness all day until she finally gave in to it.

It was her sixteenth birthday. She should be thrilled. This was the year so many things changed for her. She'd get her driver's license. Her dad would allow her to go out on car dates with boys. Her parents would let her take the part-time job at the movie theater that was perfect for her—free movies and popcorn! Her life was moving forward. Finally, she could walk away from childish things and take her first steps toward adulthood.

But she was unable to fully enjoy the moment without remembering that George couldn't. Reaching into her pocket, she pulled out her phone and fired up the flashlight app. It was that or risk breaking her neck, tripping over a headstone. She knew the way to

George's grave by heart in the daytime, but in the dark, the cemetery seemed foreign.

Using the bright beam to guide her, she followed the narrow footpath around the Harrison family's section. Then she passed the crying angel that marked where three generations of Arnolds had been laid to rest. Vivi told her Anne Arnold had bought the statue of a life-sized weeping angel with her arms extended toward Heaven after the death of her son, Bruce, during the Vietnam War, over sixty years earlier. She'd had it erected next to Bruce's grave.

The concrete sculpture had scared Jade when she was a child. The large angel was overwhelming with her wings tucked close to her body, her face distorted with pain. Now the figure didn't seem so forbidding. With age and awareness, Jade could relate to the sheer desolation and loss captured in the stone. She didn't bother to shine her light on the angel tonight. It would feel too much like dragging her own pain out of the shadows. Some things were better left in the dark.

Turning, she found the lane that led her to George. Leaning closer, she used the phone's light to read the two names etched into the headstones that stood side by side. The cold granite was as familiar to her as the smell of Vivi's chocolate chip cookies or the softness of her mother's hair on her cheek when she hugged Jade goodnight or the loud, boisterous sound of her father's laughter.

She briefly touched her Grandma Hollister's gravestone before moving on to George's. He was the one she'd come to see tonight.

Jade sank down to her knees in the damp grass, trying not to shiver as the chill assaulted her, creeping through her body. Only a fool came to a graveyard in the middle of January. If her father discovered she'd snuck out, she would begin her sixteenth year grounded until the cows came home.

"Hey, George." The greeting came out as a whisper. For some reason, the night demanded a sort of reverent silence she didn't feel obliged to observe during the daytime. She'd come to visit her twin brother's grave before, but usually she was with her mother as they replaced the flowers in the permanent vases that stood on the granite slabs. She'd never come alone, never had the opportunity to speak aloud all the things she wanted to say to him.

"Happy sixteenth birthday, Georgie. You missed a great night. We went out to dinner at O'Doyle's Restaurant. I know you've never been there, but it's my favorite place to eat in town. I had the fried chicken plate with mashed potatoes and gravy. You would have loved the chicken. It was crispy and greasy and so good. All the aunts and uncles and cousins came. Vivi was there too. I told Mom I wanted something small with just the family. Stupid me. Nothing's ever small with our family. We filled the whole restaurant. Even so, it was fun."

The knees of her jeans were getting wet, the cool moisture from the grass touching her skin. Luckily she was always hell on her clothes, so her mom wouldn't think much of the stains when she threw this pair of pants in the laundry bin.

"I didn't want a big party like that swanky thing Hope had back in May where we all had to dress up."

Jade shuddered when she recalled the fancy dress she'd had to wear. She'd felt ridiculous and uncomfortable the whole night.

"Sienna suggested we have a sleepover, like we did on her birthday, but I didn't want that either. I really just wanted to spend tonight with you."

Jade swallowed heavily, trying to dislodge the lump forming there. "I miss you, George. Sometimes I pretend you didn't die, that you've been with me all these years. I don't think you would have just been my brother. You would have been my best friend too. I'm sure of it. I wonder how different my life would have been with you here. I've lived the past sixteen years feeling like part of me was missing, like there's this big hole inside me that's empty, that's never gonna fill up. I hate it. It pisses me off."

She closed her eyes, beating back the same fury that surfaced whenever she thought of the injustice of her brother's death.

A twig snapped nearby. Jade jerked, standing quickly to flash her light toward the sound.

"Who's there?" She cursed the tremor in her voice. She was so stupid to venture to the cemetery alone. Her parents didn't even know she was out of the house.

"I'm sorry," came a deep voice from the shadows. "I didn't mean to disturb you. I wasn't expecting anyone else to be here."

She waved her phone around until she found the speaker. He lifted his hand to shield his eyes from the bright light. Compton Pass wasn't so large that she didn't know most people, if not by name, then at least by face. Unfortunately, she couldn't see his because it was hidden.

She moved the light until the brunt of the beam shone on his chest and he lowered his hand. "Hey, I know you. You're Liam Harrison. Your parents own the farm next to my family's ranch." His family was famous for their rodeo livestock, contracting to some of the biggest rodeos in the state.

Liam nodded. "You're one of the Compass girls, right?"

She grinned. She and her cousins, Sienna, Hope and Sterling, had worn that nickname since the day they started kindergarten. Apparently, four rowdy Compton cousins all entering school together had made an impression on the teacher. Where one of them was, the other three were never far away, so Miss Lacey had lumped them together and called them her Compass girls.

Of course, Jade figured turnabout was fair play. She and her cousins had done the same thing with the Mothers, their playful moniker for Jade's mom, Leah, and her aunts Jody, Cindi and Lucy.

"I'm Jade Compton."

Liam frowned. "The sheriff's daughter?"

"Yeah."

"He know you're out here alone?"

Damn. Jade tried to decide how to play this. It was a pain in the ass being the *only* daughter of the *only* lawman in town. While her dad, Sawyer, had a reputation as being a strict but fair sheriff, his overprotectiveness when it came to his little girl was fairly well known.

"Um...sort of."

Liam chuckled. He walked closer, and she noticed the bouquet of red roses in his hand. Mercifully, the moon had burst through a break in the clouds, allowing her to flip off her flashlight. While she didn't know Liam personally, she'd seen him around town. He'd been the captain of the football team his senior year, though Jade had been five years behind him, too young to know him from school.

But she knew him well enough to realize he wasn't a threat to her. Unless he told her father about catching her in the cemetery in the middle of the night.

He leaned down to read her brother's name in the granite. "George Compton?"

Jade nodded slowly. "My twin brother."

Liam glanced at her. She braced herself for the

pity she expected and was surprised when instead she found understanding. "Happy birthday."

She smiled. "Thanks." Touched by his kindness, she pushed her luck and confessed, "My dad doesn't know I'm here."

"Yeah. I didn't think so."

Something about his tone told her Liam wouldn't sell her out.

"I'd appreciate it if you'd—"

"I'm not going to tell on you, Jade."

She breathed a sigh of relief. "Thanks. Again."

Liam pointed at the grave. "You come here by yourself often?"

She shook her head. "No. I always come with my mom. Tonight I just had some things I wanted to say to George alone. That probably sounds dumb to you."

"Not at all."

"He died in childbirth." It was an inane thing to say. That much was clear from the inscription on the grave. "It was a rough delivery. My mom started hemorrhaging. The doctor was able to save me, but George didn't…"

Her words drifted away. Vivi was the only adult in her life who'd been willing to tell Jade about the night she was born. Jade had asked her grandmother point-blank a couple of years earlier and instead of receiving the standard "some things went wrong" response she'd always gotten from her parents and aunts and uncles, Vivi sat her down and declared her old enough to know the truth. She'd explained about the uterine rupture and her mother's hemorrhaging. In order to stop the bleeding, the doctor had been forced to perform a C-section, then a hysterectomy. George hadn't made it.

Liam disrupted her thoughts. "I'm surprised George is buried here. Don't the Comptons have a burial plot on the ranch?"

Jade nodded. "Yeah, but my family lives in town, so Dad can be close to the station. Vivi said my mom took my brother's death really hard. My granddaddy JD died just before my mom got pregnant, then her mom—my Grandma Hollister—had a massive heart attack four months before George and I were born. In the course of one year, my mom lost three people she loved."

"Damn," Liam whispered. "I can't imagine."

"I know. Me either. Vivi told me Mom sort of fell apart in the hospital, begged my dad not to take her baby so far away." Jade closed her eyes and imagined her mother's desolation, then she recalled the concrete angel. The statue stopped being scary the day Vivi explained why George was buried in the church cemetery instead of on Compass Ranch. Since then, whenever Jade looked at the figure, she saw her mother's face, felt her pain. "They buried George here next to Grandma Hollister. Seemed fitting, considering he was named after her."

Liam looked at the headstone next to George's. "Georgia Hollister."

Jade grinned. "After Mom and Dad found out they were having twins, they decided to name us after the parents they'd lost. My dad has a bit of a twisted sense of humor, so they named George after my grandma and me after Granddaddy Compton."

Liam smiled. "Jade is for JD? That's nice. I only know of your grandfather through reputation, but something tells me he would have loved having you as his namesake. Here." Liam pulled a rose from his bouquet. "A birthday present for your brother." He handed her the flower.

She appreciated the gesture. Turning, she placed it on top of her brother's grave.

"And one for your grandma." Liam plucked

another flower from the bunch and placed it on Grandma Hollister's headstone.

"Thank you." Curiosity finally won out. "Who are the flowers for?"

Liam's expression darkened, sadness replacing the humor that had been there only seconds before. "Celia."

"Oh. That's right," she whispered as recognition dawned.

He nodded. "Compton Pass isn't such a big place. I'm not surprised you know the story."

Celia Woods had been killed in a car accident a month earlier as she was traveling home from Denver. Apparently she'd gone to the city to pick up her wedding gown when a drunk driver crossed the median on the highway and struck her vehicle head on, killing her instantly. The Mothers and Vivi had rallied around the distraught Woods family…and her fiancé, Liam.

"You came to put flowers on her grave." The midnight visit was incredibly romantic and terribly sad.

Liam glanced away from her, looking up at the moon. "Today was supposed to be our wedding day. I tried to get here all afternoon, but I just couldn't face…"

Jade understood. While her pain had dulled with time, Liam's loss was fresh, unbearable. "But you did make it. You're here now."

He shrugged, and she wished there was some way to erase the shame he obviously felt at being too upset to visit Celia's grave. According to her mother, Liam and Celia had been high-school sweethearts, madly in love from the time they were seventeen.

"I'm sorry." Small, meaningless words, but they were all she had to offer.

He looked at her once more. "It's okay, Jade. I thought I was hanging in there these past few weeks, holding it together. Today…"

He paused. Jade's stomach ached as she recognized the anguish in his tone.

"Today…the bottom fell out."

"I think it's really sweet that you came to bring her flowers."

"Tell you what. Why don't you finish up your talk with George while I go deliver these to my bride? Then I'll come back and walk you home."

"Oh, you don't have to do that. I'm perfectly capable of—"

"Either I escort you home so I know you got there safely or I'm snitching on you. Which will it be?"

She narrowed her eyes, despite the fact she was ninety-nine percent sure he was bluffing. To be honest, she was happy to wait. Until he had arrived, she'd thought she wanted to be alone. She'd been wrong. Having someone with her who understood made the night seem less desolate, less dark. "I'll wait."

"I'll only be a few minutes."

She reached out and touched his arm. "Take your time. Say what you need to say. I'm not in any hurry."

He nodded, then disappeared into the shadows.

Jade wasn't sure how long he was gone. She'd knelt once more. The words that had been trapped inside her for sixteen years suddenly free and flowing easily. She told George everything—about Mom and Dad, Vivi, the cousins. She shared everything written on her heart and more than a few secrets she'd never uttered aloud to anyone. She'd only just run out of words when she heard Liam's footsteps on the path.

"Ready, kiddo?"

She nodded, then rose and fell into step beside him.

Pain was etched in his face, and she could see from his red eyes he'd been crying. She didn't speak.

Instead, she walked next to him, hoping her presence made him feel less alone.

When they arrived at her house, he turned to her. "It was nice to meet you, Jade."

"You too. Thanks for walking me home."

"My pleasure. Happy birthday."

She waved as she backed away from him. "Maybe I'll see you around some time."

He grinned. "Maybe you will."

He didn't leave as she walked along the side of the house. She could feel his gaze on her when she hoisted herself up on the lowest branch of the tree outside her bedroom window. She wasn't sure, but she thought she heard him chuckle as she climbed the tree skillfully—it wasn't her first trip up the trunk—then raised the window she'd left cracked and crawled back into her room.

Once she was inside, she leaned out and found him still standing there, her silent guardian. He returned her wave before walking back the way they'd come.

Chapter One

Eight years later

Jade cursed the tap as it sputtered, leaving more foam than beer in the icy mug she was filling. "Hey, Bruce. The goddamn Bud Gold tap is fucked up again."

Bruce scowled at her. "Nice language, Jade."

"Bite me."

Bruce had some nerve, calling her out for her foul mouth. She'd learned most of her more colorful four-letter words from him.

To prove her point, her boss came behind the bar, muttering, "Son of a mother fucking cock-sucking bitch."

She shot him an *I told you so* look when he pulled down the lever of the tap and was spurted by a large glob of foam. He narrowed his eyes and grunted. "I don't need to hear your lecture again."

She'd been after him to replace the antiquated set-up behind the bar for a couple years. Nobody dealt with kegs and taps anymore, but Bruce was a creature of comfort for whom change came hard.

Hopefully, he wouldn't be able to fix the thing and they'd get the Bottoms Up system she'd been lusting after since she started bartending at Spurs. No matter how many times she explained to Bruce that it would fill the cups from the bottom, quickly, efficiently and without too much head, he just rolled his eyes and said he didn't need that fancy-schmancy shit in his place. Bruce prided himself on running an old-fashioned redneck bar.

Regardless, Jade knew it didn't matter. Keg taps would become obsolete and he'd have to come over to her way of thinking eventually. That or he'd do as he had been threatening for months and sell the place to someone else so it would be their problem, not his.

Sienna and Daniel had actually tried to convince Jade to buy Spurs. She'd laughed at the suggestion, but every now and then, she considered all the improvements she could make and was tempted.

After several minutes of cursing and futzing with the ancient tap, Bruce looked at her. "I'm going to have to run out to my truck to grab some tools. Hold down the fort."

Jade nodded, then glanced around the place. It was Friday night, which meant a full house. Dorian Whitacre and his brothers had set up their instruments and were playing a fast country song—loudly. The dance floor was packed with ranch hands and roughnecks kicking up their heels and celebrating the beginning of the weekend. Any time the Whitacre brothers performed it guaranteed a big crowd.

A quick peek in the back room proved every pool table had already been claimed. She saw Liam bent over, lining up a shot. If she weren't working, she'd challenge him to a game. Though she'd never beat him, she had definitely come closer than any of the yahoos he was currently fleecing. While hustling wasn't strictly allowed in Spurs, Bruce usually turned a blind eye. He sold a hell of a lot of beer to the guys in that back room, so he wasn't about to bite the hand that fed him.

Liam had become a regular at Spurs in the past

few years. She'd been surprised when he started showing up on Friday nights shortly after she'd been hired. Sienna insisted he'd taken up playing pool simply because it gave him an excuse to hang out at Spurs to keep an eye on her. Jade had dismissed her cousin's supposition as a load of bullshit.

She figured that, like most of the cowboys in Compton Pass, Liam liked to kick back with a cold one at the end of a long week and blow off some steam. Whenever he wasn't shooting pool, he'd find a woman to dance with. Jade had watched him leave with more than a few of the local single ladies at the end of the night and he certainly wasn't keeping an eye on her as he sashayed out the door.

Sometimes she'd ask him about his dates, but Liam was always evasive, claiming it was a casual thing or a one-night deal. He hadn't had a steady girlfriend since Celia. Jade wondered if he'd ever love anyone like he'd loved his fiancée. It was sweet in a very sad way.

For the past eight years, they had a standing date, meeting at the cemetery just before midnight on her birthday. She'd visit George while Liam took flowers to Celia. Usually they met at the gate to the churchyard. After they'd spoken their peace to the cold headstones, they'd meet up once more at the entrance. When she still lived at home, he'd walk her back to her parents' place. Now that she lived on Compass Ranch, he'd escort her to her motorcycle, where they'd say goodnight and head home on their own.

Jade wished he'd find someone who could make him happy. He wasn't a bad-looking guy, with his dark hair and eyes. His tan skin reflected a life lived mostly outside. He constantly sported a five o'clock shadow and the crinkles around his eyes betrayed his penchant for laughter. Plus he'd definitely treat a woman right.

He'd been raised a country gentleman, never failing to open doors, pull out chairs and tip his hat for women. She had offered to set him up with a couple of her friends—even her cousin Sterling—but Liam had just laughed and informed her he was perfectly capable of finding his own dates.

Over the years, Liam had become one of her best friends. Even though she had still been in high school when they'd met, he'd never acted like she was an annoyance or in the way, though she knew she got on his nerves more often than not. She laughed way too loud, cussed too much and didn't have a problem sharing her opinions on most matters.

A scuffle near the bar caught her attention. Jade turned just in time to catch Roscoe Hutchins rearing back to throw a punch at Bucky Dorsey.

"Jesus. Same shit, different day," she muttered as she walked around the bar and shoved her way through the crowd forming around them.

Rhonda Barker was standing between the two men, who were arguing with more bluster than muscle.

Jade struggled not to roll her eyes. "Break it up, guys. If Bruce comes in here and sees you starting this shit again, he'll ban you for life, Roscoe."

Roscoe pointed an angry finger in Bucky's face. "I'm not leaving here until I've taught this little shithead to keep his hands off my girlfriend."

Bucky laughed. "Your girlfriend came on to me. Maybe you need a few lessons in fucking, Coe."

Roscoe lunged forward again, but this time Jade and Rhonda were both there to push him back. Not that Jade sensed he was trying too hard to get to Bucky. His actions were clearly more for show.

What a joke. Jade had been walking the razor's edge of an explosion for weeks, looking for an outlet. Looked like she'd just found it.

"Enough!" Jade yelled. "Goddammit, you people are annoying. Roscoe, at some point in your miserable life, you're going to have to figure out that Rhonda is a slut."

Rhonda, who had been holding Roscoe back, dropped her hands and turned toward Jade, fury written on her face. "Hey! Who are you calling a slut?"

"Oh, I'm sorry, Rhonda. Does that word not work for you? What would you call a woman who sleeps around? Whore? Tramp?"

Roscoe, shocked by the catfight erupting in front of him, stopped trying to get to Bucky. "Damn, Jade. Take it easy. It was just a little misunderstanding."

Jade poked her finger into Roscoe's chest. "No. It wasn't. The two of you start this crap up every freaking weekend with a different guy. Rhonda cheats on you, you pick a fight with the loser of the week and—"

"Hey," Bucky interjected. "I'm not a loser."

Jade flipped her hands as if waving away a fly. "Go away, Bucky. You haven't changed a bit since high school. You're still thinking with the same head. It's a shame it's not the one with a brain in it."

"Who pissed in your cornflakes this morning?" Bucky turned around and walked back to his usual spot at the bar.

"Listen, Jade," Roscoe started, "I think maybe you should just—"

She raised her finger to cut him off. "Shut up. Where was I? Oh yeah, and after you *pretend* like you're going to kick someone's ass, you get booted out of the bar. I don't know…maybe this is how you and Rhonda get off, but I'm sick and tired of the game. If you want to get pissed at someone, why don't you start yelling at this faithless bitch? Or better yet, grow a pair and dump her ass!"

"You little cunt!" Rhonda lunged for her, and

Jade was ready. She'd been itching to punch something for days. Unfortunately Roscoe grabbed Rhonda, pulling her away as Jade felt strong, familiar arms wrap around her waist, lifting her from the screaming woman with ease.

"Hey!" She fought against Liam's hold as he started dragging her out of the crowd.

"Easy, kiddo. I think you need to go outside to cool off for a minute."

Jade tried to shake off Liam's grip, but she was no match for his strength. The man was built like a brick shit house, towering over her by at least six inches. "Let go of me! They started it and now I'm going to finish it."

Bruce came through the back door just as Liam lifted her up and tossed her over his shoulder like a sack of potatoes. "What the fuck is going on in here?"

Liam gestured toward the bar with a tilt of his head. "The Rhonda and Roscoe show."

"Goddamn idiots." Bruce slammed down his toolbox as he headed toward the crowd. "Take a few minutes to rein it in, Jade, and then get your ass back behind the bar. I'm kicking those jackasses out once and for all. I've had it with this shit."

Liam carried her out of the bar as she beat on his back, his ass, anything she could reach. Once they hit the parking lot, she expected him to put her down, but he didn't.

"You finished?" he asked.

Liam had a way of talking to her sometimes that made her feel like she was a two-year-old throwing a temper tantrum. It never failed to calm her down. And piss her off.

"Yeah, asshole. I'm done."

He placed her on her feet and crossed his arms.

"What the hell was that about?"

"I don't like being manhandled, Liam."

"I'm not talking about that." He pointed toward the bar. "I mean you and Rhonda. You know what she's like. Hell, everybody in town—Roscoe included—knows what she's like."

"So we're all just supposed to sit back and let her and her stupid boyfriend continually create this weekly drama? What's it for? Our entertainment? Because it's getting old. And boring."

"All I'm saying is Roscoe is well aware of Rhonda's affairs, but he's never going to dump her. And Rhonda, for all her faults, seems to genuinely love Roscoe."

Jade scowled and started to argue, but Liam continued speaking. "She just loves sex with other guys more."

She laughed. "A lot more."

"They're harmless, Jade. A Compton Pass tradition. Rhonda cheats, Roscoe picks a fight, Rhonda cries, Roscoe forgives her and life goes on. Half of the guys who sleep with Rhonda want the fight with Roscoe more than the sex with her. Gives them a way to get their rocks off *and* work off some aggression."

Jade released a long sigh. "I know that."

"Then why the strong words?"

She shook her head. "I don't know. I've been feeling edgy lately. Restless. I mean, look around, Liam. Is this all there is to life? Every single day is déjà vu and not in a good way. It's like I'm trapped in the horror movie that is my life, forced to endure the same stupid things over and over and over again."

Liam frowned. "So what are you saying? You want to leave Compton Pass?"

"No." Jade closed her eyes wearily. "This is my home. I don't want to leave. My whole family is here and with Vivi's memory getting worse..." Her words fell away as her shoulders slumped. She was in a funk. Usually life didn't get her down, but for the past few months, she'd struggled to shirk off her constant state of unhappiness. The worst part was she didn't really know what was bothering her. She was suffering from what Vivi called a case of the blues. And she had it bad.

Liam reached out to touch her arm. "Maybe you're just bothered about your grandmother's illness. Alzheimer's can take its toll and you've been watching Vicky's decline for a couple of years now."

She shrugged. "I *am* worried about Vivi, but I don't think that's what's wrong with me. Not really."

"Then what?"

"I'm stuck in a rut. I work at the ranch. I tend bar here. I hang out with my cousins and you. I eat the same breakfast every day. The same damn lunch. I break up the same ridiculous redneck fights week after week. I'm coming out of my skin. It makes me want to do something crazy, wild, impulsive."

"What else is new?"

She shot him a dirty look that he ignored.

"Fine, kiddo. Be impulsive."

She released a quick snort. "Easier said than done. I'm Jade Compton, the sheriff's daughter, one of the Compass girls. Sometimes it feels like I have a thousand eyes on me—all watching out, ready to protect me the second I step one tiny toe over the line into anything that could be potentially dangerous. I'm living my life swaddled in freaking Bubble Wrap."

Liam laughed. "I don't know about that. It seems to me you've managed to do some damage. Weren't you the girl who got pulled over by her father for going a hundred and twenty on her motorcycle?"

"Yes. And I caught holy hell for it too. Uncle Silas is still reading me the riot act for that, and it happened nearly six months ago."

"Liam leaned against Bruce's car. Her boss always parked in the alley. "I bet he is. That is one man I'd never wanna piss off."

Jade blew out a long breath and tugged at her T-shirt. "It doesn't help that it's a gazillion degrees this summer. I'm tired of being hot. It's like I'm living in a pool of my own sweat with my clothes sticking to my skin every time I step outside."

"Attractive image. Thanks for sharing."

She grinned. Liam always knew how to talk her out of her anger. No matter how mad or annoyed she might be, Liam managed to calm her down. "Okay. You win. I'm finished bitching."

"So what's your plan for getting out of your depression?"

She lifted her shoulders. "I don't know. I guess I'll just have to come up with something spontaneous and reckless. Maybe I'll jump my motorcycle over Beyer's Creek. I can sell tickets and put on a flashy pantsuit. I can even come up with a cool stunt-girl name like Jumpin' Jade."

"Selling tickets hardly makes it an impulsive act."

She could tell he wasn't taking her seriously and her pride kicked in, his *whatever* attitude rubbing her the wrong way. "Then maybe I should do something even more stupid."

"And what would that be?" His casual tone tweaked her temper and made her long to wipe the smug smile off his face. As always, she acted without thinking.

"This." She gripped his shirt in her hands and tugged him close, kissing him roughly. She felt him stiffen with surprise, the response appeasing her enough that she released him with a superior laugh. Served him right for dragging her out of the bar and then not believing her when she threatened to do something insane. He was her friend. The least he could do was play along when she was in a mood.

His eyes narrowed, pleasing her even more. Liam was a hard person to shock, so it felt good to shake the cocky man up.

"Oh my God, you should see your face right now, Liam."

Her laughter died when Liam grasped her cheeks in his large palms and pulled her forward.

"Apparently you need a lesson in recklessness, Jade."

"Wha—" She didn't have a chance to ask what the hell he was doing before Liam placed his lips on hers and kissed her. Shock held her still for a full minute as Liam took charge of her mouth. His grip was firm, directing her face this way and that as he pressed her lips apart and started exploring her mouth with his tongue.

Part of her was compelled to shove him away. She'd only meant the kiss as a joke. This was Liam, for God's sake. For eight years, he'd been her best friend. They didn't kiss.

But damn if he didn't know his way around a mouth. Jade lifted her hands to his shoulders. Her initial intention had been to push back, but once her fingers found the firm muscles on his upper arms, she decided to indulge in a little exploration of her own.

Liam twisted them until she was pressed against Bruce's car, his body leaning into hers. One of his hands left her face, caressing its way along her neck, briefly touching her breast before latching on to her waist. He used his grip to tug her lower body even closer to his.

Shit. Liam had a hard-on. For her?

She didn't turn him on. Did she?

He pressed her more firmly against the vehicle, and Jade let him take the lead, take over. She wasn't a meek lover—at least she never had been in the past—but she was definitely allowing Liam to hold the reins, following along as he pushed her arousal higher.

He slipped one hand beneath her T-shirt, his fingers stroking the sensitive skin there. She moaned, the sound captured by his mouth. Too much more of this and he'd have her purring like a kitten.

His hand moved higher, cupping one of her breasts tightly in his large palm. He squeezed, slowly applying more pressure until Jade thought her body would spontaneously combust from the heat. Then he dug his fingers beneath the lace of her bra. She knew what he was seeking. When his fingers closed around her nipple, her head flew back as she searched for air.

Liam growled—an actual fucking *growl*—and tugged her face back to his, his lips claiming hers once more. Then…he pinched her nipple. Roughly.

Jade jerked against him, wondering if she'd ever felt anything more painfully beautiful. "Harder," she breathed against his lips.

Liam hesitated for only a second, then he gave in to her demand, his fingers tightening around the taut nub. Her panties were wet, soaked, and for a brief moment, she actually considered saying to hell with it, tugging them and her jeans down, and demanding Liam take her—Spurs drunks be damned.

She could feel just how thick his cock was as he pressed against her. He was large and long. She wanted to see…and feel…more.

Of Liam?

What was she doing?

She shoved on his shoulders, dragging her lips away from his, despite how much she really, *really* wished she could keep kissing him. Liam pulled his hand out from under her shirt.

She swiped at her mouth, the slight taste of the beer he'd been drinking still lingering on her lips. "What the hell was that?"

Liam gave her a cocky, nonchalant grin. "You said you wanted to do something spontaneous. That seemed a hell of a lot less dangerous than a motorcycle stunt."

With that, he turned and headed back to the bar. For a minute, she wondered how he was walking so casually with that fence pole in his pants. How could he pull himself together so quickly?

When he opened the door, he looked over his shoulder at her. "You coming, kiddo?"

Her legs felt like they were sunk in quicksand, but somehow she managed to put one foot in front of the other until she stood next to him. She opened her mouth to say something, but she didn't have a clue what. So instead, she shut it and kept walking.

Was the kiss Liam's attempt at one-upmanship? Teaching her a lesson for teasing him? She wouldn't put it past him to employ such a trick. After all, they both possessed an unhealthy amount of pride. She'd started the game and he had definitely finished it. Asshole.

But that didn't really explain the erection he'd made damn sure she felt.

No, it was a lark. Just a joke. It had to be that, right?

Consoling herself with the idea Liam was jerking her chain, she took a deep breath and dismissed the kiss completely.

Returning to her station behind the bar, she began filling drink orders and consciously *not* looking toward the back room.

She managed to ignore the temptation to take a

peek for all of twenty minutes. Then her willpower dried up and she glanced over to the pool tables.

Liam was leaning against the far wall, pool cue in hand. But he wasn't watching the table or the game. Instead, he was looking right at her.

Her stomach fluttered at the intense—holy crap—hungry expression on his face.

Nope. It hadn't been a game.

And Liam had lied.

The jump on her motorcycle would have been much less dangerous.

Chapter Two

Liam looked across the campfire and grinned. Jade and one of the Compass ranch hands, Jameson, were standing off to the side of the campsite, throwing knives at a tree trunk where Sterling had etched out a makeshift bull's-eye. They'd turned it into a competition—each of them shedding a piece of clothing if their throw was farthest from the center. Jade hadn't missed the spot yet, much to Jameson's chagrin. The poor hand was down to his boxers and still hadn't wised up enough to know he should quit now.

Sterling retrieved the knives from the thick trunk, handing Jameson's to him and shaking her head. "You sure you don't want to concede?"

Jameson looked around the campsite, then down at his boxers. "Maybe I should. There are a lot of ladies present."

Jade scoffed. "There's no one here except us Compass girls, so the ladies excuse is flimsy at best."

"Hey," Sienna called out from her spot next to Daniel at the campfire. "I'm a lady."

Jade rolled her eyes, letting her *sure you are* expression answer for her. "Just throw the knife, Jameson. Want to see if Sterling was exaggerating about what you're packing under there."

"Hey now, that's getting a bit personal." Jameson glanced at Sterling.

Sterling laughed. "You have a bad habit of losing. I gave you an out on strip poker too, but you insisted on taking it right down to the bitter end."

Jameson laughed and cupped his cock. "You didn't think it was bitter later that night, Sterling."

Jade gestured to the weapon. "Gross. Just throw the knife, J."

Jameson took one last look around the campsite, obviously searching for support. His gaze landed on Liam.

Liam shrugged, refusing to be pulled in. "You're the one who made the bet."

Clayton shook his head, jumping into the conversation. "Don't get too excited, girls. I saw his hairy ass in the bunkhouse too many times. Was damn relieved when Wyatt made lead ranch hand and we scored our own place. You're not gonna get much of a show."

"Lucky you," Boone grumbled. "I still have to see it every day."

Liam laughed. This was the second June in a row he'd headed off into the mountains with Jade, her Compass girl cousins, as well as Daniel, Wyatt, Clayton, Boone and Jameson. It was a fun group. They'd loaded the horses up with tents, food, too much beer, and this year, Boone had insisted on dragging his guitar along. Situated next to a small lake, the campsite provided cool water, beautiful views and complete privacy. They could crank up their music as loud as they wanted and get rowdy without anyone complaining.

Jameson sighed, realizing he was trapped. "Fine." He threw the knife. Resigned to his fate, he didn't even bother to aim. He hit the bull's-eye. "Holy shit!"

Jade laughed loudly. Her noisy, animated laughter had pierced Liam's eardrums many times in the past. Jade didn't do anything quietly and for years he'd considered wearing earplugs whenever she was around just to dim the sound a bit. Lately, though, he noticed it didn't seem to bother him as much. In fact, he'd started to like the sound.

Dammit. He needed to get his head out of his ass and start thinking logically. Jade had given him a wide berth since his impulsive kiss outside Spurs last weekend and he'd been reading himself the riot act for it ever since. He still wasn't sure what had gotten into him that night.

He'd woken up the next morning with a slight headache and had considered chalking it up to one too many beers. However, it wasn't anything that innocent. Jade had laid down a challenge with her teasing kiss, and being the arrogant fool he was, he'd reciprocated, intent on giving her a taste of her own medicine.

He'd intended to simply kiss her, but somewhere along the line, the plan backfired until his cock was rock-hard and his hand was in her bra.

Now Jade kept eyeing him with a suspicion he didn't care for, all because he'd let things get way out of hand.

At some point tonight, he'd pull her aside. They'd clear the air, laugh about it and then life could go back to normal, with them firmly standing in the *just friends* realm. There was no way in hell he was going to change *that* status. He couldn't date Jade Compton. She'd run roughshod over him, drive him nuts, wear him out with her crazy antics.

And that loud laugh. That blow-your-eardrums-out, joyful, husky, sexy laugh.

He reached for another beer.

Sienna pulled the hot dog she was roasting on the

flames toward her to inspect it. "Here's another hot dog if anyone's still hungry."

Daniel reached for it, but Sienna pulled it away quickly.

"Another one, Daniel? That will be your fourth."

Daniel laughed, then snuck a quick kiss from his fiancée. Deepening the embrace, Daniel distracted Sienna just enough that he was able to claim the hot dog.

She pulled away from him when she realized what he'd done. "Hey. You tricked me."

Daniel shrugged, unrepentant. "I'm hungry, See."

"You realize the tuxedo has been ordered. You better fit in it come August."

The date for Daniel and Sienna's wedding was set. It would take place at the end of the summer. Liam had jokingly referred to this outing as one of Daniel's last chances to make a break for it before he was trapped forever. Told his friend he could hide in the mountains for the next thirty years or so until it was safe to come out.

"It'll fit. Don't worry."

Jade and Jameson reclaimed their weapons, finished with the game. Jade walked over to him. "Thanks for loaning me your knife, Liam."

He took it. She tried to turn and walk away from him, but he grasped her wrist and tugged her toward the log where he was sitting. "Take a load off, kiddo. I want to talk to you."

She resisted his pull briefly, then gave in. "What's up?"

"I haven't seen you much this past week. You didn't stop by the ranch on Tuesday."

Shortly after their meeting on her sixteenth birthday, Jade had ridden the horse her uncles kept for her on Compass Ranch over to his spread. She was fascinated with the training of bulls and broncs for the rodeo and he had allowed her to watch him work with the animals, answering all her questions. After that, she'd become a regular at the Circle H Ranch.

Nowadays, just a few miles spanned the distance between his house and the one Jade shared with her cousin Sterling. Originally all four Compass girls had lived in the small cabin tucked in the woods. Their fathers had built it for them—probably so the overprotective dads could keep a close eye on their rambunctious adult daughters. However, Sienna and Daniel had already moved into the new house Seth and Jody had given them as a wedding present and Hope had moved in with her boyfriends, Wyatt and Clayton.

A path had formed between Compass Ranch and his home as Jade rode her horse over to visit. He'd finally put a gate in between the two properties four years earlier, so Jade would stop jumping the fence. She rode her horse too fast as it was. The last thing he needed was for her to get thrown mid-leap with no one around to help if she was hurt.

She stretched out her legs, not bothering to look in his direction. "I've been busy."

It was on the tip of his tongue to apologize for kissing her, but he wasn't sorry he'd done it. No matter how ill-advised that kiss had been, his body told him it wouldn't mind expanding on the experience.

She studied the fire intently. He'd been worried about her lately, well aware of her recent depression.

He'd marked it down to a combination of stress over Vicky's illness and Sienna's wedding until she'd mentioned being bored with her life. Jade had never been the type to play by the rules. She always colored outside the lines. Obviously she was hungry for adventure. Unfortunately he knew damn well what that meant. While she'd joked about jumping the creek on her motorcycle, part of him suspected she was seriously considering doing it. She was too reckless, and he wished he could find a way to help her rein in all that energy without her running the risk of breaking her neck.

He had noticed a hint of Jade's wildness on the very first night they'd met. After all, what sixteen-year-old girl sneaks out of her house in the middle of the night to visit her dead twin brother? Most girls her age wouldn't have dreamed of stepping foot in a cemetery alone after dark. And yet, there was Jade, sitting next to the grave as if it was the most natural thing on earth. He'd been impressed by her bravery, but even more so, Liam had been touched by her obvious love for the brother she'd never known. He'd heard some of the things she'd spoken to George and promised himself he'd keep an eye on her for the brother who couldn't be there.

"I could have used some help with that new bull, Fearless."

She eyed him, distrustfully. "You were going to let me work with him?"

He nodded. "Sure. Why not?"

"Is he ready to be ridden?"

Liam laughed. "Not yet. And not by you. I've got plenty of dumb rednecks working on my ranch who don't mind the risk of breaking their necks."

"I don't mind that risk either."

"It's not gonna happen, kiddo, so forget it."

She harrumphed and fell silent once more.

Most folks in town looked at Jade and saw a hard-ass bitch, a tomboy through and through. She cursed like a sailor, drank like a ranch hand and drove way too fast on her Harley, while sporting tatty jeans and a leather jacket. If he ever learned that her hair had seen a curling iron, he'd eat his hat. Jade didn't do fancy hairstyles or wear makeup. She didn't need to. With her wavy blonde hair, bright blue eyes and wholesome complexion, she was a natural beauty.

Over the years, as Liam got to know her better, he'd come to understand the tough exterior didn't reflect the inside accurately. Underneath it all, Jade Compton was as soft and sweet as butter in the sunshine. She cared deeply about her family and friends. She had never failed to show up at the cemetery on her birthday, though for the past few years he wondered if her appearance there was more for his sake than hers. She'd made him chicken soup when he'd gotten a killer case of the flu last year and she spent every single Wednesday afternoon, without fail, visiting with her grandmother.

Liam could always tell which Wednesdays had been good—with Vicky lucid and telling stories about JD—and which had been bad. There were too many afternoons nowadays where Vicky couldn't remember who Jade was. It was on those days Liam watched Jade struggle to fight back tears. And yet, he'd never seen her let a single one fall.

Time to break the ice. He wasn't a fan of the cold shoulder. Especially when it came from her. He'd actually missed her this week.

"You don't have to keep avoiding me, Jade. I don't have any plans to corner you and kiss you again anytime soon."

For the first time since she sat down, she actually looked at him. "Why did you do that?" There was no accusation or anger in her tone. Instead, she seemed genuinely confused.

"You kissed me first."

She gave him a dirty look. "That was a joke and you know it."

He did know it. But he was hard-pressed to

explain why he'd taken things so far. She deserved an answer, but he didn't have one to give her. Not one that made sense anyway. The truth was…something had sort of sparked for him. She'd pressed her lips to his, and for the first time, he wasn't seeing the young girl he'd befriended in a cemetery. Suddenly she was an attractive woman whose touch made his cock hard, whose soft lips felt just right pressed against his, who made him want to do dirty, dirty things to her. The blinders had fallen away, revealing a Jade he hadn't noticed before.

Of course, there was no way in Hell he was confessing all that to her, so he went for the cop-out. "I have no idea why, Jade."

The worst part was he wanted to do it again. However, given her reaction, it was obvious she didn't want a repeat performance.

"It was weird."

He laughed, spying a way to put them back on solid ground. "No, it wasn't. It was fucking hot. You're not a bad kisser. I could probably give you a few pointers on some ways to improve, but overall—"

"Not bad? Are you kidding me? I rocked your world, cowboy. And don't even bother trying to deny it. I felt what you were packing in your pants. You wanted me."

Liam shook his head, relieved that the conversation was traveling familiar paths. Taunting and teasing was second nature to them. Mercifully, the kiss hadn't destroyed that. "Don't flatter yourself, kiddo. I'd had a few too many beers and you have to admit, there were some hot buckle bunnies at Spurs that night. I'd been sporting a woody for close to an hour before I kissed you."

"You go to hell for lying, Liam."

"Well, I guess we'll never know the truth. It was

a one-time thing and I'm not planning to go in for seconds."

"Good."

Her grin made him long to erase some of the smugness he saw there. With another kiss.

Not a good idea. He took his hat off and swiped the sweat at his brow. "Goddamn, it's hot."

Jade released a long breath. "You can say that again. It's only mid-June and it's already a scorcher. Wish we could get some rain to cut through the heat."

"Weatherman said we might be in for a bit of a drought."

"Great. If the grass gets any drier, we'll be fighting brushfires before too long."

He and Jade both volunteered as firefighters, pitching in to help whenever a fire got out of hand or was too big to be contained by the two full-time firemen. "Yeah. I was thinking the same thing. Two more weeks of this heat and we wouldn't have been able to have our campfire."

Wyatt and Clayton threw a couple more logs on the fire and for a long time, they all sat, passing around a bottle of Jack, chatting and listening as Boone strummed his guitar. Night had fallen, the brightness of the fire casting shadows around the campsite.

After nearly two hours, Sterling stood and tugged at her T-shirt. "I'm freaking hot. Who's up for skinny-dipping?"

"What do you say, See? There's no way we're going to fall asleep tonight unless we cool down first." Daniel rose, reaching down to help Sienna stand.

"You're just saying that so you can see me naked." Sienna started to unbutton her jean shorts.

"Sweetheart, it's my plan to see you naked every night for the rest of my life. That view never gets old."

Daniel and Sienna clasped hands and walked

along the path, away from the campsite.

Wyatt, Boone, Hope and Clayton hopped up as well.

"I'm in." Jameson pulled off his shirt and rushed to catch up to Sterling as the others walked to the lake. Within seconds, they'd disappeared into the darkness.

"You game?" Liam wished his cock wasn't suddenly thickening at the thought of a naked Jade. What was the matter with him?

Maybe it was a lack of sex. It had been a few months since he'd hooked up with anyone. Daniel had accused him of sprouting morals, suddenly wanting a relationship rather than one-night stands, but Liam was fairly certain that wasn't his problem. He'd tried to forge a happily-ever-after once before with Celia and all he'd gotten for it was unbearable sadness and an ache in his chest that had taken years to fade. As far as he was concerned, bachelorhood might be a bit lonely, but it was far less painful.

Ordinarily skinny-dipping was Jade's idea and she would have been the first one in the water. However, despite the fact they'd cleared the air, he sensed her hesitation. Finally, the heat won.

She lifted her long blonde hair away from her neck in an attempt to cool off. "Daniel's right. It's going to be hot in that tent. Race you?"

He sprinted off the log, gaining a two-step lead before she'd even managed to stand.

"Cheater!" she yelled from behind him.

He kicked off his shoes and pulled off his T-shirt as he ran, tossing it on the path. Then he started tackling the button on his jeans. Shucking them and his boxers at the shore, he jumped into the chilly water without bothering to look back.

He expected Jade to be hot on his heels, but when he didn't hear her, he turned to look for her.

The others had swum out further and were currently engaging in an all-out splash war.

He scanned the darkness, then found her. Jade remained by the shore, struggling with her jean shorts.

"Problem?" he called out.

"The damn zipper is stuck. Oh, there. Got it." She tugged the shorts down. She was completely naked. Though the moon was covered with a thin veil of clouds, enough light escaped to allow him to see her clearly. They weren't strangers to skinny-dipping and Jade had never been modest. In the past, he'd averted his eyes because it seemed like the right thing to do.

Now he couldn't look away as she walked deeper into the water. And closer to him.

By the time she reached his side, the water was to her shoulders, her bare body hidden from view beneath the murky surface.

Every drop of moisture in his mouth evaporated. He swallowed heavily. Despite the cold lake water, his cock was hard as steel.

Jade smirked, and he wondered what she saw in his face. Whatever it was, he didn't doubt for a minute he'd given himself away. "There aren't any buckle bunnies around now."

Figured. She was trying to prove a point. And damn him if she hadn't.

Even so, he had as much pride as the next guy. "So?"

"So take a picture next time. It'll last longer."

He wanted to deny how much the sight of her naked body affected him, but considering the fact all the blood needed to operate his brain was in his cock, he was finding it difficult to speak at all.

"Listen, Jade. Obviously things got out of hand the other night and some lines got blurry."

She nodded. "Yeah. I guess they did."

"Probably doesn't help that neither one of us has gotten laid in a while." There were very few secrets between him and Jade. It wasn't unusual for her to fill him in on her sexual escapades. Plus she was usually manning the bar at Spurs and had a front-row seat when it came to watching him slip away with his Friday-night hookups, not that he'd indulged in any of those lately.

"You losing your touch with the local ladies?"

Jade might be knocked back by her confusion, but she never fell down. They'd been skirting the edge as they tried to get things back on track tonight. God bless her, Jade kept returning for more, feisty as ever, ready to put things to right.

He flicked a handful of water at her. "You don't have to worry about my abilities. I can handle myself just fine."

Jade never turned down the opportunity for some roughhousing. She returned his splash with interest. For several moments, they continued to pummel each other with giant handfuls of water, the game a familiar one.

Then Liam dove under for a sneak attack, swimming toward her as she tried to escape. He managed to get a grip on her ankle, tugging her under with him, while Jade squirmed, trying to break his hold. They came up for air at the same time, Jade laughing loudly.

Not finished with the battle, she pushed herself up on his shoulders in an attempt to jostle him under the water once more. It was a move she'd used countless times in the past, as they often wrestled and fought while swimming.

This time, it wasn't the action that caught him off-guard, but the way it made him feel. Her bare breasts grazed his chest as she shoved him down. Then his face was there, inches from her tight nipples. The cool water did nothing to calm his lust. His cock was hard and given Jade's close proximity, that fact was going to be impossible to hide.

He gripped her waist in an attempt to push her away, but Jade misread his intent, taking it as a dare to continue. She followed him, tried to drag him under the water again as her laughter and squeals continued. She was oblivious to the effect she was having on him. Why wouldn't she be? He'd never felt this way during their earlier encounters.

Before he could think better of it, Liam pulled her bare body against his. Her nipples poked at his chest as his cock rested against her stomach.

His strong hold and undeniable arousal shocked Jade into stillness. She panted, winded from their exertions, and her face flushed.

"Liam?"

He didn't reply. Common sense reared its ugly head, screaming at him to let her go, but a wrecking ball couldn't have moved him away from her at that moment. It felt too good to hold her. Too right.

Jade's hands rested, unmoving, on his bare chest. "You're not helping to refocus the lines right now."

He knew that. "Sorry."

"No, you're not. But this has to stop, Liam. I'm not sure what's going on between us, but I think we need to take a big step back. We've been friends for a long time and neither one of us has had a relationship in years. We're both feeling a little lonesome, so it's probably normal for us to think we're attracted to each other."

He didn't *think* he wanted her. He *knew* he did.

He also knew she was dangerous. To his lifestyle. To his peace of mind. Jade Compton was a handful on a good day. On bad days…watch out. Any man who thought he could take on a wild filly like her needed to have his head examined.

Despite all of that, he still didn't release her. "I'm not lonely, Jade." He wasn't. "Are you?"

She considered his question. "No. I don't think I am."

He released her and moved away. Something was changing inside him and if he didn't get away from her soon, he was going to do something they may both end up regretting.

He glanced toward the campsite. "I'm getting out of the water."

She nodded but remained where she was as he started walking toward the shore.

Distance. All he needed was space. And time to figure this out. Jade was high-strung, opinionated, wild as a summer storm. While there was a chance she might bend her will to his in the dark of night, he had no illusions that she'd march to anyone's beat but her own in the bright light of day.

What man in his right mind would sign on for something like that? He sure as hell couldn't.

Could he?

He bent down to pull his jeans on, feeling her eyes on his backside. His cock thickened even more.

Fuck. He didn't need time *or* space *or* his head examined.

Danger be damned.

It was already too late for him.

Look out, Jade Compton.

He was about to give new meaning to the term *reckless.*

Jade made no move to leave the water. She'd give Liam a chance to put his clothes on and return to the campsite. If she stalled long enough, maybe he'd be in his tent by the time she walked back.

Things were too crazy between them right now. It

was as if her world had been turned on its ear. She'd never felt a sexual attraction to Liam before that damn kiss, but she'd spent every night this week with her vibrator, driving herself to orgasm after orgasm while imagining his face. It had lit a fire inside her that wouldn't be quenched, no matter how many times she masturbated. Maybe it was time to find a ranch hand, some hot stud to help her fuck Liam out of her system.

Problem was the only man she wanted was Liam.

What the hell was she supposed to do with that? She wasn't going to indulge in an affair with Liam. That would be stupid. And strange. And wrong. Wouldn't it?

"Hey. What are you doing over here by yourself?" Sterling swam up to her.

"I wasn't alone. Liam was with me. He just got out."

"What's up with you two today?"

Leave it to Sterling to notice. Her cousin was far too observant. Always had been. Sterling had an amazing talent for reading people's faces or body language and knowing how they felt—whether they were scared or sad or nervous.

Jade started to say nothing, but changed her mind. Maybe Sterling could help her understand what was going on. "We kissed last weekend."

Sterling's eyes widened. "Like kiss-kissed?"

Jade nodded. "Open mouth, tongues, roaming hands, hard cock pressed against my stomach. The works."

"Whoa."

Jade sighed. "Yeah."

"I mean, I guess it's not surprising. I've noticed the sexual sparks between you two."

Jade felt as if her cousin had knocked her to the ground. "What the hell are you talking about?"

Sterling tilted her head. "There's always been sexual tension there, but neither one of you ever seemed to notice it. Plus, let's face it, the two of you fight like cats and dogs. I just figured you were happy with the status quo and not looking to mess up an awesome friendship. Was it a good kiss?"

Jade bit her lip. "It was incredible. I can't stop thinking about it."

Sterling grinned. "Well, hot damn."

Jade raised her hand to halt where she could see Sterling's X-rated mind taking her. "I'm not having sex with Liam."

"Why not?"

"Because it's Liam."

Sterling rolled her eyes and made a buzzer sound like Jade was on a game show. "Errrr. Lame excuse. Try again."

Jade fell silent for a few seconds before admitting the truth. "That's the only reason I have. It's exactly what you said. I would never risk losing Liam's friendship for a few minutes in the sack."

"I've heard rumors about Liam in the bedroom and I can promise you it would be a hell of a lot longer than that."

"You know what I mean."

Sterling gave her a strange look that Jade couldn't begin to interpret. "I'm not sure I've ever seen you show this kind of restraint."

"What do you mean?"

"You're acting so out of character. You never think things through, never hesitate, never act like…forgive me…a girl."

Jade narrowed her eyes, feeling foolish, but offended nonetheless. "I'm not acting like a girl."

Sterling laughed. "Of course you are. You just said the kiss was great. Let's face it. If this were any other guy in the world, you wouldn't have stopped there last weekend. You'd have dragged the man home and fucked him until the sun came up. And I'm pretty sure you wouldn't be standing in this lake, naked and alone, if it wasn't Liam who'd managed to get your panties in a twist."

"I'm not wearing any."

Sterling shot her an annoyed look.

Jade couldn't argue with her cousin. Sterling was right. Jade wasn't exactly known for curbing her desires. If she wanted something, she took it. Thinking didn't usually come into play. Yet all she'd done this past week was think. And think. And think.

It was driving her batty.

"So I'm just supposed to throw away eight years of friendship and fuck Liam's brains out until we get tired of each other. You said it yourself. We fight all the time. We wouldn't make it a day and a half before we were at each other's throats."

"Oh, Jade. You're always such a pessimist. What if the two of you hooked up and it was so great, you fell in love and lived happily ever after?"

Jade scowled. "You're drunk. You know perfectly well I have no plans to ever get married."

Sterling giggled. "I'm sober as stone, you grumpy bitch. You know what could cure this bad mood of yours? Sex. Sweaty, sleeping-bag sex."

"I'm sharing a tent with *you*."

"You have no imagination."

Jade rubbed her forehead. "I'm getting a headache. I think I'll turn in early."

Sterling glanced over Jade's shoulder. "Okay. I'll come with you. Looks like everyone's getting out now anyway."

Jade noticed the others heading back to the campground. Jade climbed out of the lake, tugged on her shorts and T-shirt, then walked with Sterling. Liam was sitting on the same log they'd occupied earlier, gazing at the fire.

Jade skirted the circle and headed straight for her tent. She said her goodnights, then before she climbed in, she glanced back at Liam.

He was staring directly at her. His face reminded her of the way he'd looked after their kiss at Spurs. It scared the shit out of her. And turned her on so much, she physically *ached*.

Time to get a grip. She gave him a dirty look before unzipping the two-man tent and crawling in. She'd been an idiot for talking to Sterling about Liam. Clearly she had picked the wrong cousin to confide in. Sterling's view of life was completely warped, so now Jade was even more confused.

She would have been better off asking advice from Sienna or Hope. Of course, both of them were so head over heels in love, she suspected their opinions wouldn't have been much different than Sterling's. Except while Sterling was telling her to go for hot sex, Hope and Sienna probably would have told her it was fate and started planning another fucking wedding.

This was insane. She was going to go to bed and when she woke up, life would be back to normal. She'd treat Liam like she always had and they would forget the past seven days. Problem solved.

Except Jade couldn't accomplish the first part of her plan. Sleep eluded her. She listened to the quiet strum of Boone's guitar and heard the murmur of voices for nearly an hour, though she couldn't make out what was being said. She'd tossed and turned so much, her sleeping bag was twisted into knots beneath her.

Finally, she heard someone at the entrance to the tent. Jade sat up, ready to warn Sterling about her restlessness, when she spotted Liam climbing in.

"What the hell do you think you're doing?"

Liam closed the zipper, then crawled into Sterling's spot. "Your cousin shanghaied my spot about half an hour ago. She and Jameson were making out like the plane was going down."

"Tough luck. You're not staying in here. Take Sterling's bag. You can sleep next to the campfire with Boone."

"And get eaten alive by mosquitoes? No thanks. This tent is fine."

"Liam—"

"I'm not going anywhere, Jade. And that's that."

Jade tried to fix her bag, flatten it again.

He watched her struggle to smooth it out for a few quiet minutes. "I figured you'd be asleep by now."

She blew out an annoyed breath. "It's stifling in here."

Liam chuckled. "No, it's not. You sure you're not just hot and bothered? Because I could take care of that for you."

Jade lay down and turned her back to him. "Go away."

"No. In fact…" Liam scooted his bag closer to hers, then wrapped his arm around her waist, tugging until he was spooning her. "I sort of like the idea of snuggling with you."

Jade sucked in a deep breath, trying to ward off her arousal. Crap. Sterling was right. She wasn't used to curbing her desires and right now it took every ounce of willpower she had not to roll over, straddle Liam's hips and scratch the itch.

So instead, she put up a token resistance, trying to break his grip. "Dammit, Liam. Really?"

Her strength was no match for Liam's and they both knew it. He trained bucking bulls, for God's sake. His muscles had muscles.

"You finished?" he asked.

His question reminded her of the back alley at Spurs. He'd asked her the same thing just before he'd kissed her.

She stilled. "Yeah."

"We're just sleeping, kiddo."

"Don't you think it's sort of perverted to hold me like this while calling me kiddo?"

He chuckled. "Yeah. Probably. I'm sure as Hell not going to deny there's a woman in my arms right now."

She was sorry she'd mentioned it. She didn't mind the nickname. In fact, she liked it.

He tugged her even closer and Jade could feel his erection against her ass through his boxers and her lightweight pajama bottoms. She wiggled to prove she knew it was there.

He laughed. "Just lay still, close your eyes and rest awhile."

"You're not going to give this up, are you?"

She felt rather than saw him shake his head. "No. I don't think I am."

"You're wasting your time. A relationship between the two of us would never work, not for the long-term."

He pressed a soft kiss to her shoulder. "You're right. It probably wouldn't."

She twisted in his arms, turning to face him. "Then why push this?"

"Because I can't stop."

She would have questioned him further, but the moon had broken free of the clouds. She and Sterling had left the top cover off the tent, both of them wanting to look at the stars. The sheer mesh sent a stream of light into their tiny space, allowing her to see his face clearly.

Liam seemed resigned to something she was only just beginning to understand. It was pointless to fight the unavoidable.

And she and Liam and sex…

Well…

It was inevitable.

Chapter Three

Liam tightened his grip on the training rope as the new bull he'd been working with kicked violently against the constraints. He was pleased with the grit Fearless had shown during his initial sessions. This bull was shaping up to be one of his best ever. If he kicked like this during competition, Fearless had a chance at going down in the rodeo history books, much like Bodacious had over thirty years earlier.

"Damn. That's one fine bull."

Liam looked over his shoulder as Daniel strolled over. Liam had been so intent on the training, he hadn't heard Daniel pull up in his pickup.

"Yeah. I was just thinking if he keeps it up, this bull could kick some pretty serious cowboy ass."

Daniel chuckled. "I sure as hell wouldn't want to ride him."

Liam released the strap on the bull and leaned against the fence.

"What are you doing over here? Isn't it a bit early for happy hour?" Daniel had moved to Compass Pass nearly three years earlier to work with Sienna's father, Seth, breeding prime horseflesh. Since then, he and Liam had become friends. They were about the same age, both cowboys with a love of sleek horses, a bottle of Jack, and a good game of pool. And they were both currently trying to figure out how to deal with one of the infamous Compass girls, not that Daniel knew of that last, more recent common bond.

Of course in all fairness, Daniel had an easier task with his Compton lady. Sienna was reliable, down-to-earth and practical. Daniel didn't have to worry about her getting into barroom brawls, challenging some roughneck to a drag race or hopping onto the back of a wild stallion. Liam had witnessed Jade do all three of those things. More than once. Which was why he should be trying to get his cock under control instead of considering the leap from *just friends* to something more.

"I'm not here to drink, though God knows I sure as hell could use one. There are too many women over on Compass Ranch with only one thing on their minds these days—me, gettin' hitched in style. I keep trying to convince Sienna to run off to Vegas, but she's not budging."

Though Daniel complained, his face betrayed him. He was head over heels in love with Sienna and there wasn't a damn thing he wouldn't give the woman. While Daniel bitched and moaned about the wedding plans, Liam wasn't fooled. He suspected Daniel was looking forward to the big day as much as the bride.

"You picked a tough family to marry into. They're great people—one on one—but damn, when you put them all together, it's like a tidal wave crashing on your head."

Daniel laughed. "You got that right. Between the *Cousins* and the *Mothers* issuing orders, all of us men are jumping around like barefoot bums on hot asphalt. We're painting shutters, planting flowers, fixing fences, tidying up the yard, hiding all the ranch equipment they think is *ugly*, which is a pain in the ass considering we need to use the tools to do our jobs. Spent nearly half an hour this morning looking for these so I could return them."

Daniel handed Liam several straps he'd borrowed the previous week. "Thought I'd better get them back to you before they went missing for good."

Liam took them and tossed them near the door of the stable. "Thanks."

"Heard through the grapevine that Jade nearly took Rhonda Barker's head off at Spurs a couple weeks ago. Surprised you didn't say anything on the camping trip. Sounds like it was quite a show."

Liam shrugged. "Wasn't much of a story to tell. They just exchanged a few words."

"Rumor has it you pulled her out of the bar before fists flew."

Daniel had been insinuating that Liam had feelings for Jade for nearly a year, despite the fact Liam constantly denied it. Ever since Daniel had decided to get married to his pretty girlfriend, he'd been determined Liam should take the same plunge. And for some insane reason, he had fixated on Jade as the top choice for Liam's future bride.

Now that he thought about it, it was probably Daniel's fault he'd responded to Jade's kiss in the first place. His friend had planted the seed so many times…it was starting to take root.

"I broke up the fight. That's all. You would have done the same thing, so don't go reading anything into it." Liam wasn't ready to confess that his feelings had changed to Daniel. Mainly because he still wasn't completely sure what he was going to do. He had some ideas of what he wanted to do, but he needed a more solid strategy than the single thing that was floating through his head right now. *Have sex with Jade.*

Jade wasn't some weekend hookup. While this

sudden physical attraction was strong, Liam knew there was a hell of a lot more to it than just that. He cared about Jade, always had. There was no way the two of them could embark on a sexual affair without emotions and history coming in to play. He just had to decide if he was willing to take the next step because God knew it was a big one and there would be no turning back—at least not for him.

With the exception of her cousins, no one knew Jade Compton better than Liam. And as such, he knew that lately she was a powder keg set to blow and any man fool enough to get close to her was bound to lose a few limbs in the explosion. He needed to proceed with caution. And that required some serious forethought and a game plan.

Daniel gave him a shit-eating grin. "Noticed you two sharing a tent on the camping trip."

Liam rolled his eyes. "Only because Sterling crept off with Jameson and stole my sleeping bag." He blew out a long breath, then asked a question he knew Daniel would think was a joke. Unfortunately, Liam needed a serious answer. "Let me ask you something. Would *you* take up with Jade Compton?"

Daniel crinkled his nose. "Hell no. Sienna's baby brother, Doug, suggested I date her when I first moved to Compton Pass. Believe me, I knew right from the beginning she was too much woman for me."

"But you think I should sign on for that? Why?"

Daniel shrugged. "I dunno. Call me crazy, but I think the two of you would be pretty good for each other." Daniel gestured to the bull standing in the pen next to them. "Face it. You don't seem to have a problem with wild beasts."

Liam wasn't sure how to respond. The words rang true. And as hard as it was for him to admit it, he was starting to think his friend was right. He and Jade fit. He'd never noticed it before, but he should have. For eight years, she'd been the one constant in his life. The problem was their relationship had evolved so slowly—from acquaintances to neighbors to best friends—he'd failed to consider there could be something more there. Somewhere over the past two weeks, one thing had become completely apparent to him. The untamed woman *did* appear to be his type.

Daniel took Liam's silence as further resistance. "Fine. You've made it perfectly clear Jade's not your type. I'll stop giving you shit about it."

Liam tipped his hat in unspoken thanks, glad to be let off the hook. He wasn't about to tell Daniel about the kiss. Or the skinny-dip that took a rather provocative turn—thank God no one noticed that. Or the fact he'd held Jade all night in the tent, savoring the way her sweet body fit against his.

"You still coming to dinner tonight? Big wedding powwow, remember?"

Liam nodded. Daniel had asked him to stand next to him as best man. Part of him thought Daniel had issued the invitation simply so he'd have backup whenever the wedding ideas got out of hand. So far he and Daniel had managed to talk the bride and her cousins out of boogying down the aisle. Apparently, Seth and Sam had done some sort of crazy two-step as they'd approached the altar to say their I do's and the Compass girls thought a repeat performance would be fun. Daniel had firmly put his foot down, insisting he was not about to make a fool of himself on his wedding day. Liam had supported him because he sure as hell didn't intend to dance either.

"I'll be there, but I'm telling you now, I don't think there's any way you're going to convince those girls to let you out of writing your own vows."

Daniel blew out a long breath. "I know. Sienna

mentioned it again this morning. I'm in trouble with that one. I mean, I love Sienna, but I don't know how the hell I'm supposed to say all that mushy-gushy stuff women love in front of everybody. I'm going to come off like a babbling idiot and I'm pretty sure I'll spend the next few years of my life taking shit from the ranch hands for sounding like such a sap."

Liam slapped him on the back and gave him a wicked grin. "Not just the hands, Daniel."

"Asshole."

Liam laughed. "I have faith in you, partner. Tell you what, we'll work on it together next weekend over a bottle of Jack. I'm sure we can figure out a way for you to say something sweet without sounding like a complete tool. What do you think?"

Daniel grinned, taking off his hat and beating the dust out of it against his jeans. It was another scorcher, the sun shining down on them mercilessly. "Sounds good. I better get back or Seth will send a posse to track me down. He gave me hell when I said I needed to return those straps to you. Said it was a lame excuse for escaping. Informed me I'd better not dawdle too long or he'd make me drive Jody and Sienna to town to pick out the design for the wedding bouquets this afternoon." Daniel feigned a shudder. "They've already been to the florist twice and both times they were there over four hours. What the hell can you do in a flower shop for eight hours?"

"I have no idea. Of course, I'm not sure I could tell you the difference between a daisy and a dandelion. Celia took care of all that stuff on her own when we were planning our wedding."

Daniel's brow creased. "I hope all these plans aren't bringing up bad memories for you."

Liam appreciated Daniel's concern. A few years ago, he probably would have struggled with the preparations, but the passage of time had eased that pain, taking it from the sharp, bullet-to-the-chest agony he'd experienced shortly after her death to a dull ache that only crept in occasionally. "I'm fine, Daniel."

As always, Daniel found a way to alleviate the heaviness of the moment with humor. "You know, I still think fate will throw a woman in your lap soon enough and when it does, you'll start jumping through all these fool hoops too. By then, I'll be on the other side, laughing my ass off at you."

Liam rolled his eyes. "Get out of here. I'll see you tonight."

Daniel climbed into his pickup and drove away as Liam turned toward the corral. He didn't bother to start the training again. Instead, he rested his chin on his hand against the top rail of the fence and let his mind wander. He glanced toward Compass Ranch.

The path between his home and Jade's was empty. Not that he was surprised. Jade hadn't made the trek to his house since he'd kissed her at Spurs. Just thinking about her had his cock twitching, thickening. It was starting to become a recurring state for him and it was chafing. Literally.

Then a scheme began to take shape. Taking a straightforward approach with Jade wouldn't work. For one thing, she'd been swearing off serious relationships since she was sixteen, insisting that marriage was something she wouldn't succumb to. He'd never questioned her decision because for too many years, he'd given up on the idea of settling down as well. After Celia's death, it seemed like he'd never find anyone he wanted to spend the rest of his life with.

Suddenly, being a part of a couple again sounded pretty damn good. Not that he was going to tell Jade that. He'd have to ease her into the idea, sneak up on her from behind. The woman had built defensive walls around herself that were ten feet thick.

He considered his trip to Compass Ranch tonight. While he was going to help with the wedding preparations, he could kill two birds with one stone. The more he thought about it, the more certain he was his plan was good.

The only thing he needed to do was persuade Jade to go along with it.

He scoffed.

Chances were slim Jade would agree to what he intended to propose, but it didn't matter.

He'd find a way to convince her.

Because there was only one thing he was confident of right now. He wanted Jade in his bed…and his life.

God help him.

Jade and Sterling laughed loudly at Jake's off-color story as Jody and Leah began clearing the dinner dishes. Liam shook his head at the packed-to-the-gills room. Considering most of the Comptons lived on or near Compass Ranch, big family meals were the norm. Even so, Liam wasn't sure he'd ever get used to the holiday-like atmosphere surrounding a simple weeknight dinner.

For Liam, the only time his family's dining room saw more than just him for a meal was at Christmas. His father had died of a massive heart attack when Liam was twenty-five, so running the ranch fell to him. The youngest of three children—and the lone son—Liam had been the only sibling still living at home when his father passed. Both of his sisters had married and moved to Denver prior to their father's passing. Liam's mother—a city slicker at heart—had decided she'd had enough of ranch life shortly after his dad's funeral. Without her husband tying her to the country, she moved to Denver as well, anxious to play the role of full-time grandmother to the three nieces and two nephews his sisters had already given him.

Which left the family homestead and business to Liam. Not that he minded. He'd known from the cradle he would never leave Compton Pass or Circle H Ranch. It was home.

"Jake," Sawyer said, his tone laced with a warning that indicated he didn't appreciate the ranch hand talking about unusual sexual positions with his daughter and niece.

"Sorry, Sheriff." Jake gave Jade and Sterling a wink. "I'll finish the story later."

Sawyer shook his head, but Liam caught the man's grin as he muttered something about it being no wonder the girls were so wild.

Seth leaned forward, capturing Liam's attention. "What's the word on this new bull I keep hearing about? He really as good as everyone claims?"

Liam grinned, perfectly aware of where Seth had gotten his information. Jade was determined Fearless was going to be the greatest rodeo bull who'd ever bucked off a cowboy.

"He's tough, but it's too early in the game to tell. We haven't had a rider on him yet."

"Even so," Jade joined the conversation, "he's definitely got what it takes. I've never seen an animal with a kick like Fearless. It's incredible."

Though he'd claimed the chair next to her at dinner, Jade had made a concerted effort at ignoring him throughout the meal, opting instead to chat with Sterling who was seated on her right.

This was the first time she'd acknowledged he was even in the room.

Liam shook his head, amused by her enthusiasm. "Jade. We've only had the strap on him. How a bull responds to that isn't always a good indicator of how he'll take to a rider."

"Fearless is going to be great. Mark my words."

Liam didn't bother to argue because he actually agreed. Jade saw the same things he did. He'd considered trying to drag her away from her job on Compass Ranch more than a few times over the years. Jade was born to work with the cattle. She'd participated in rodeos throughout her childhood and high school and even had an offer to ride with the amateur circuit after graduation, but she'd turned it down.

Jade, like him, was a homebody at heart. They'd both flap like fish out of water if someone tried to take them out of Compton Pass.

Lucy came into the dining room. Silas rose and pulled out a chair for her, while Colby walked toward the kitchen. Her husband gave her a sympathetic smile. "I'll get your plate, Lu. Jody's keeping it warm in the oven."

Lucy had skipped eating with the family, opting instead to sit next to Vicky's bed. There were times when Vicky's memory failed and being surrounded by the large group of relatives left her disoriented, agitated. Vicky Compton was one of the strongest women Liam had ever met. He could only imagine how frustrating it was for her to suddenly struggle to remember the names of her children and grandchildren.

Lucy smiled when Colby set the plate in front of her. "Vicky is asleep."

"She doin' okay?" Silas asked.

It was rare to ever see any weakness on Silas's face, but Liam had glimpsed the sheer desolation in the oldest Compton son's eyes quite a few times in the past year.

"She's fine. Once I got her away from all the

noise and hubbub, she settled right down. I read to her until she fell asleep."

Sienna toyed with the stem on her wineglass. "I shouldn't have asked everyone to come here for the wedding meeting. We could have had dinner at my house."

Sterling shook her head. "All of us eating in your tiny kitchen? That would have been fun to watch. Don't do this, See. Vivi was fine this morning and looking forward to the big meal. Sometimes she's okay in this situation. We just have to play it by ear."

Jade had confided in Liam shortly after Vicky's diagnosis that it was her grandmother's desire to live out the remainder of her years in an assisted living community rather than at home. So far, the family had managed to convince her to remain on the ranch, each of them taking a turn caring for Vicky. He knew Jade hoped they'd be able to keep Vicky with them forever, but on more than one occasion, her grandmother mentioned moving to the nursing home.

Each time, Jade would excuse herself, escaping either on her motorcycle or horse—always racing away as fast as her mode of transportation would carry her.

Liam had vowed that when her grandmother finally disappeared from them forever, either physically or mentally, he would be there for Jade the same way she'd stood by him after his father's death. When he looked back now, he realized he wouldn't have made it through the funeral if not for Jade's constant, comforting presence.

As various family members started drifting to other parts of the house, Liam decided the time was right for his talk with Jade.

Sienna and Daniel were discussing music for the ceremony with Leah. Colby and Silas kept Lucy company as she ate her dinner. Jody and Hope were in the kitchen preparing dessert and coffee, while the menfolk escaped to catch a bit of the baseball game—the Cardinals were taking on the Reds.

Jade started to follow Sterling into the living room, but he captured her hand.

"Hey," she said, resisting as he tugged her down the hallway. "Liam. I want to watch the game."

"No, you don't. You hate baseball. Said it's the equivalent of watching paint dry."

He didn't bother to release her hand until he'd dragged her out onto the screened-in back porch. Since the rest of the family was in the front of the house, it provided them a quiet place to talk. And privacy.

He closed the door behind him, positioning himself in front of it. He didn't trust her not to try to leave.

She crossed her arms and gave him an annoyed look. "What do you want?"

"Why are you ignoring me?"

She scowled. "I'm not."

He tilted his head. "Don't fib, Jade. It makes me want to spank that pretty ass of yours."

Her spine stiffened at his warning. He couldn't help but noticed the flush creeping along her cheeks—though he had no idea if it was interest or anger driving the color. If he wasn't careful, Jade was likely to give him a swift knee to the balls.

Regardless of that, he felt the need to test the waters. His sexual needs ran a bit toward the extreme. Jade's reaction to his rough kiss and the hard pinch he'd given her nipple gave him hope they shared the same proclivities.

He'd engaged in several BDSM affairs in the years since Celia's death, releasing the darker desires he'd always tried to stifle when he was with his fiancée.

"Tell me the truth or I'll pull down those tight

shorts of yours and give you a taste of my brand of punishment."

When Jade's eyes darkened with lust, it felt like his world shifted, tilted. Then he realized it was just the opposite. Too many pieces were finally falling into their proper place.

Jade recovered quickly. "Who the hell do you think you're talking to? You've lost your mind, Liam Harrison. First that kiss in the parking lot, then that power play in the tent where you insisted on holding me all night, and now you're threatening to *punish* me? Where is this coming from?"

He took a step closer, the alpha in him provoked when Jade backed away. She matched his pace—the two of them engaging in an odd version of chase—until he trapped her against the sidewall. He lifted his arms and caged her in.

Liam studied her response to his capture—on the off chance he was wrong about Jade's sexual tendencies. He didn't want to scare her, and if he was mistaken, he needed to rein in his dominant side.

Her breathing had accelerated and, God bless the USA, her nipples had tightened, the buds straining against the thin cotton of her T-shirt. She gave him a dirty look through heavy-lidded eyes that didn't fool him for a minute. She was turned on by his dominance.

And it pissed her off.

Jade was stubborn as a mule and mean as a pit bull if cornered. He knew her well enough to know he'd have to let her believe she was calling the shots…at the beginning. Once he got her under him, that tune was going to change damn fast. The image of Jade tied to his bed floated through his mind. His dick twitched.

"I've been thinking about your dilemma."

She frowned, her gaze darting to the door that would deliver her back to the safety of her family's house. He leaned closer, letting her know she wasn't getting away from him.

"What problem?"

He stroked her cheek with one finger. Jade shuddered. "You're bored. Looking for some excitement. I'd like to offer my services."

She considered his proposal, then gave him a superior grin. "You'll let me take a spin on Fearless?"

He barked out a laugh at her attempt to distract him. "Good God, no." She'd been after him for weeks to let her ride the wild creature. Hell would freeze over before he ever agreed to let her do something so dangerous and stupid. Jade knew it, but that didn't keep her from pestering him about it.

"Then there's nothing you have to offer me." Jade raised her hands to his chest and tried to shove him away. He didn't budge. Liam had never really let her see his strength, never tried to overpower her. Until now.

She licked her lips. Liam tried to decide if the action was an invitation…or perhaps nerves. Most likely it was both. "Cut to the chase, Liam. Spit it out."

"You know what I want."

She narrowed her eyes, her face proving she knew exactly what this conversation was about. "Say it anyway."

He didn't hesitate, didn't see any point in hedging. "Sex."

Jade laughed and tried to dodge under his arm. He lowered it just in time, holding her firmly in place. She tried to struggle, but she was no match for him.

"You're manhandling me again."

"I'm trying to have a serious conversation with you, Jade."

"This is ridiculous. Did you fall off a horse and hit your head? This is me you're talking to. Jade. We're friends. We don't fuck. You have the bimbos at Spurs for that."

"This isn't just about sex. Do you want to hear my idea or are you going to keep playing the coward? For someone who claims to want to go wild and be impulsive, you're acting awful skittish."

The taunt had the desired effect. If there was one thing Jade couldn't resist it was a dare...or an insult to her courage.

"Fine." She stopped trying to escape, dropping her arms. She was pretending to humor him, but her body was too tense, a live wire ready to spark. He was getting to her. "Let's hear it."

He lowered his hands until they rested on her waist, then he tightened his grip, hoping the hold would remind her of their kiss in the parking lot. "You said you feel like you're coming out of your skin, tired of the same-old, same-old. I think I have the remedy."

She placed her hands on his wrists. He thought she'd try to pry his hands off, but instead, she loosely clasped them. It was a defensive movement plain and simple. She'd allow the hold...but nothing more. "And your answer is sex? Wow. Typical male response. Fucking cures everything, right?"

"You've been pushing the limits lately, Jade. Driving your motorcycle too fast. Picking that fight at the bar. Daniel told me about your spin on that wild horse of his. The one he's fighting like the devil to break. He said you got thrown pretty hard and you were lucky you weren't hurt."

"That was over a month ago. And Daniel acts like an old woman, gossiping and making stories sound twenty times worse than they really were."

"You're hell-bent on putting yourself in danger, all in the pursuit of excitement. And none of it has worked, has it?"

Jade didn't respond, but she was definitely listening.

"You're still depressed, floundering for a way to break free. So I propose you try something different. There's a better way to change up the daily routine, to get your motor revving."

She shook her head. "I can't believe you're suggesting this. You don't seriously expect me to have sex. With you? Just because I'm bored?"

He nodded. "Actually, I do."

"And after those five minutes are over, what do you advise I try next?"

He laughed at her insult, then moved closer. "It wouldn't be just sex."

She frowned. "I don't understand."

"I'm offering you something more intense than just vanilla sex. Something I think you'd like to try."

Her eyes darted to the door once more. Yep. She was in panic mode. "I don't have a clue what you're talking about."

"You like it rough, don't you? You like your pleasure laced with pain."

Jade's chest rose and fell rapidly as her breathing increased. "Don't be silly."

"I can give you that. And more."

"Like what?"

Liam struggled not to grin at her question. While she was feigning disinterest, her body was betraying her.

"I'm going to take over in the bedroom. Dominate you. You'd like that, wouldn't you?"

She shook her head, but her eyes didn't meet his. She was careful to look anywhere besides his face. "I'd kill any man who tried to tell me what to do. You included."

He was tempted to call her a liar, but it was

obvious she wasn't ready to give in just yet. He'd have to peel back a lot of layers before Jade would accept her true nature. And his. He'd never bothered to drop the shield, to show her the man aching to get out because he'd bought her tough-girl act and decided there wasn't a submissive bone in her body. Now...he was starting to think he'd been wrong.

Actions were more potent than words. Liam cupped her face, leaning down to kiss her. Jade didn't bother to pull away. Instead, she met him halfway, her lips accepting his.

For several moments, he kept his kiss slow and gentle, amused by Jade's efforts to control it. She tugged at his hair, pressed her lips harder against his, stroked her tongue along the inside of his mouth.

There was no doubt about it. He had definitely freaked her out and now Jade was determined to regain the upper hand. Prove to herself—and him—that she wasn't what he thought.

She was grasping at straws. He let her direct the kiss for a few minutes, then he gripped her face between his hands and pushed her away. She tried to draw him back toward her, but he resisted easily.

"You finished?"

She blinked rapidly a few times. "I thought this was what you were after."

"I want you, Jade. And believe me, no one's more shocked by that fact than me. You're nervous about what I'm offering and I understand why. There's a lot at stake here. So what if we take some of the pressure off it?"

"How?"

"What's the biggest reason stopping you from sleeping with me?"

Jade's response came so quickly, he didn't doubt for a minute it was sincere. It was also the answer he'd been expecting. "I don't want to lose you. My sexual relationships tend to implode pretty quickly."

Liam chuckled. "You can say that again. Have you ever dated a guy for longer than a month?"

"Careful, pot. I don't think you wanna call this kettle black. I've never seen you take the same girl out more than a handful of times."

She had a point. For a long time, he'd compared every woman he dated to Celia and he'd never found anyone who measured up. So he'd indulged in meaningless sex with women who didn't mind exploring the facets of BDSM with him. While those nights had helped him uncover a part of him he'd resisted, they hadn't filled the part of him that longed for companionship. He hadn't met anyone who held his interest or challenged him.

Jade did. She'd captured his attention in the cemetery years ago and he'd yet to become bored by her antics or her smart-talking ways.

Luckily he'd anticipated her concern and had come up with a way to buy himself some time to alleviate her fears while drawing her closer to him, giving her time to recognize what was all-too-clear to him now. "We'll put limits on the affair. We'll go into this knowing when it will end."

A crease formed in Jade's forehead. "That sounds logical, but I'm sure there's a hornet's nest in there somewhere."

"Neither of us is dating anyone. And I know for a fact you want me."

Jade tilted her head. "God, you're a cocky bastard."

He gave her a knowing grin. "Need me to prove it?"

She shook her head quickly. "No. I have no idea how you'd try to confirm something like that and I don't wanna know."

"I'm in a rut too, Jade. Kissing you was the most exciting thing I've done in months."

"You realize how pathetic that sounds, right?"

He chuckled.

She released a long breath. "But if we're being entirely honest, the same holds true for me."

"Here's what I want you to do. Anytime you experience that antsy feeling, that desire to do something reckless or crazy, call me. Or better yet, come to my house."

"Why would I do that?"

Liam didn't bother to answer. Instead, he tugged her T-shirt over her breasts, then dragged her bra down until he'd exposed her. If her uncles and dad ventured out to the porch, he was a dead man, but his brain was having trouble convincing the rest of him that mattered.

She fought to cover herself. "Liam. My family is—"

Her words died abruptly when he bent over and sucked one of her nipples into his mouth roughly. He didn't bother to hold back. It was time to draw the real Jade out of hiding.

He nipped at the tight nub, enjoying her gasp of pleasure, the way her hands tangled in his hair. Then he repeated the same forceful sucking, alternated with sharp bites, on the other breast.

"Oh my God," she whispered. "Liam. That feels so…" Her words drifted away as he continued to suckle her.

Her hands held him firmly to her, not that she needed to bother. He had no intention of releasing her. He would continue this assault until she agreed to his offer. He wanted Jade in his bed and he was prepared to fight dirty if necessary.

He continued to play with her breasts for several

minutes, driven to rougher touches, firmer squeezes, harder bites by Jade's soft cries and pleas for more.

When he sensed she was reaching a precipice, he pulled away and tugged her clothing back in place. He had to be careful not to overplay his hand. "That's why you'll call me. That's what I'm offering. Sex without strings. The chance to dip your toe in the water of bondage, submission and anything else you want to try."

He sensed the word *yes* hovering on her lips. Her desire for what he was offering was almost palpable. Unfortunately, she wasn't finished digging her heels in. She shook her head—though he wasn't immediately sure if she was denying him or trying to shake herself back to awareness. "We're friends, Liam. I don't want that to change."

"That's solid. We're putting boundaries on the affair to protect it."

Jade blinked rapidly, her sharp mind finally managing to emerge from the haze of arousal. "For how long?"

Jade was sincerely concerned. He'd never known his impulsive, fly-by-the-seat-of-her-pants friend to resist something she wanted. For now, he needed to make her believe this was just a brief affair, a way to scratch the itch, without endangering the friendship.

Liam wanted to lay it all out on the line, to tell her he wouldn't be satisfied with anything less than forever, but that would be tantamount to pounding the nails in his own coffin. Jade would never embark on a sexual relationship with him if she knew exactly how much he wanted. He'd have to ease her into that realization.

So, for now, he'd try to win her heart and convince her they fit together while offering her a safe haven called casual sex and experimentation. "End of the summer. Our last night together will be the evening of Sienna and Daniel's wedding."

Jade grinned. "A summer fling?"

Liam wrapped his arm around her shoulders and pulled her close. He sensed she was wavering. Time to move in for the kill. "The hottest fling ever. What do you say?"

She fell silent for several moments as Liam held his breath, praying for the answer that would put him—and his cock—out of his misery. "Can I think about it?"

He frowned, wanting to push her for an answer now, but pressure wouldn't work with Jade. Her concern was genuine. And he was touched she would put her own desires aside to protect their friendship. In fact, he understood her fear because he shared it.

Liam couldn't imagine a life without Jade in it. She'd been scarce these past two weeks and the time had dragged by at a snail's pace. He'd been miserable without her loud laughter, her boundless energy, her over-the-top enthusiasm for just about anything and everything that happened at Circle H Ranch.

"Fine. Yeah. Take a couple days to consider it. But don't wait too long."

She scowled at what must've sounded like an ultimatum on his part. He didn't mean it that way, but his libido was seriously fucking with his brain.

"That's not a threat, Jade." He grasped her hand and pulled it to the front placket of his jeans. She didn't resist when he pressed her palm against his covered erection. "It's a plea."

He expected her to make a joke, to tease him. Liam was surprised when she added more pressure to her touch, stroking his dick through the denim with enough strength to make his eyes drift shut, cause his jaw to lock. Christ, he was horny. He couldn't remember the last time he'd wanted a woman this much.

For several quiet moments, she merely stroked him. Then her hand disappeared.

He opened his eyes to find her studying his face. He wasn't sure what she saw there, but the anxiousness in her gaze lifted, a small smile covering her face.

"You promise me that no matter what happens this summer, after Sienna's wedding, things will go back to normal?"

He nodded, the lie tasting bad on his lips. "Sure."

"I'll give you my answer soon."

This time when she pushed against his chest, he gave way, allowing her to return to the house. Rather than follow, he walked over to the screen door and stared out into the night. He needed a few minutes to sort out his thoughts…and to coax his cock back into down-boy mode. Returning to the house with Jade—and a hard-on—while her father and uncles were around was the equivalent of waving a red flag in front of a herd of raging bulls.

He was pretty damn sure Sawyer wouldn't approve of the proposition he'd just offered his only daughter. Hell, he didn't feel all that great about it himself. When he'd come up with the idea this afternoon, it had seemed like the perfect solution to his dilemma. He'd offer Jade the security of a casual affair, while slowly showing her exactly why they should embark on a longer engagement.

Now…there was too much that could go wrong.

And God help him if it did.

Because losing her was not an option.

Chapter Four

Jade wiped the counter as the last few stragglers settled their tabs with Bruce. She frowned when she noticed her boss rubbing his stomach. He'd been doing that a lot lately.

"My gut aches tonight."

"Did you go to the doctor yet?" she asked when Bruce walked behind the bar.

"I don't need some hack poking and prodding at me. I'm fine."

Jade closed her eyes and prayed for patience. She didn't find it. She leveled a glare at her boss. "Goddammit, Bruce. Are you fucking kidding me? You've probably got an ulcer in there eating away at your stomach. Get some medicine or you'll drop dead of stubbornness."

Bruce started to argue, then winced. "Stop yelling at me, Jade."

"I will when you go see someone and get this fixed." She closed her mouth, realizing she was fighting a losing battle. "Why don't you go on home? I'll finish cleaning and lock the doors on my way out."

Bruce nodded, a sure sign he felt bad. He never left her alone at the bar late at night. He glanced around and Jade followed his gaze. She caught sight of Liam standing outside the building, talking to Jameson. A couple of the Compass ranch hands had over-imbibed. Liam was probably making sure they had a sober driver.

Bruce walked to the front door. "Hey, Liam. You mind hanging out while Jade closes up tonight? I'm cutting out early."

"Sure thing." Liam said something to Jameson, then returned to the bar.

"What the hell, Bruce? I'm perfectly capable of shutting the bar down by myself." Jade had managed to avoid Liam since his racy proposition for a sexy summer fling three days earlier. She knew he was waiting for an answer, but she still wasn't convinced a couple months of getting laid were worth throwing away eight years of friendship. Regardless of Liam's assurances that they would be fine, she knew better.

Sex would change everything.

Ultimately, if it had just come down to that, she would have said thanks but no thanks.

However, Liam was offering more. He'd dangled something she wanted desperately even though she feared crossing over a line that would be the equivalent of opening Pandora's box.

Submission. She had felt that desire tugging at her since the night she'd lost her virginity, yet she'd never given in to it. Never trusted anyone enough to experiment, to explore, to submit to. She'd never allowed herself to discover if her feelings were genuine or mere curiosity.

She trusted Liam. Completely. He'd never hurt her, never take things too far. In fact, it was perfect. Jade suspected Liam would never fall in love again. He'd given his heart to Celia years ago, so she didn't have to worry about emotions gumming up the works.

For three days, she'd struggled to decide. She

hadn't mentioned his proposal to her cousins because they didn't know about her attraction to the concept of submission. It was the only secret she'd ever kept from Sienna, Hope and Sterling.

She wasn't sure how they would respond to that admission. Would they take it in stride or see it as some sort of weakness? Deep inside, she knew they'd love her even if she sprouted an extra head. After all, Hope was in a committed relationship with Clayton *and* Wyatt, an honest to God threesome, just like Silas, Lucy and Colby. None of the cousins had blinked twice when Hope fell for two handsome cowboys.

However, she could only imagine her cousins' faces when they discovered Miss Independence, take-no-shit-from-anyone Jade longed to submit to a man in the bedroom. Hope had never hidden her yearning to find a relationship just like her parents, so it came as little surprise when she did. Meanwhile, Jade hadn't given her cousins any indication of how dark her desires ran.

Now she would be trapped with Liam and no closer to deciding what to do. "Are you listening to me, Bruce?" she repeated. "I'm fine doing this on my own."

Bruce ignored Jade's protestation. He walked behind the bar and dug into a drawer for his car keys.

Jade studied her boss's face and took pity on the man, letting the subject drop. Bruce was pale and sweating profusely. She wondered for a moment if she should take him to the hospital.

"Are you okay?" she asked quietly when Bruce turned to leave.

He turned around and gave her a weak smile. "Yeah. Got a bottle of Maalox by my bed. I'll drink some of that before I go to sleep. If it still hurts in the morning, I'll go to the doctor."

Wow. He was sick. "All right. If it gets too bad

Summer Fling

tonight, call me. Okay?"

Bruce patted her on the shoulder. "You're a good girl, Jade. Don't worry about me. I'll be back to normal in a few days."

Jade pretended to shudder. "Damn. Don't know if I should root for you to get better or not? Normal's not exactly pretty on you."

Bruce chuckled. "Little minx." Then he looked at Liam, who'd claimed a stool at the bar and was watching their interaction. "Keep an eye on her. Don't like her walking through that dark parking lot alone."

Liam nodded. "I'll take care of her."

Bruce walked out the back door, leaving Jade and Liam alone in the quiet bar.

"I'd tell you I don't need a babysitter, but I know it would be wasted breath."

Liam gave her a smile that was too charming, too handsome. While she'd always acknowledged his hotness factor, it had never taken her breath away like it did lately, which was another reason she was hesitant to accept his offer. Sexual attraction was one thing, but falling for Liam would be outright insanity. She wasn't about to play second fiddle to a ghost. Not that there was much of a competition. Celia had been beauty incarnate, graceful, intelligent, soft-spoken. She was no doubt the ideal girlfriend.

Jade? Not so much.

"I'm not going anywhere. You need help cleaning up?"

Jade appreciated the offer. "I've taken care of everything out here. Just need to pop into the backroom and tidy up there."

Liam rose from the stool and followed her to the back. They spent a few minutes picking up trash, carrying beer bottles to the recycle bins, wiping the tables. Once they had the room in order, Jade started to head back to the bar.

Liam stepped in front of her, blocking her exit. "What's your hurry?"

He'd been so quiet, she'd actually started to think she would escape tonight without having to give him an answer.

"It's late. I'm tired."

Liam gave her a knowing smile. "You're part vampire, Jade. I've seen you close here only to head over to Compass Ranch for an all-night poker game with the hands too many times to buy that excuse."

"I don't have an answer for you." Maybe if she just came clean, she could get out of here quicker. Too long in Liam's presence was hazardous to her state of mind. She could already feel her pussy growing wet, her nipples budding. Her heart was racing, her lungs tight, and if she loosened her grip on the reins even just a little bit, she'd have Liam on his back on one of those pool tables while she straddled his hips and rode him like a mustang.

Liam—damn him—didn't respond. Instead, he let his gaze wander down her body slowly, then back up. She was uneasy with his uncanny ability to see things she was fighting like the devil to hide. "Then you don't have to give me one."

She frowned, confused. "What?"

He reached out and cupped her cheek in his large palm. "I'm not going to force you into anything you're not comfortable with. If you haven't decided yet, that's fine. Just be warned that I intend to work overtime to convince you to say yes."

Jade swallowed heavily, wishing her body didn't go into overdrive every time he touched her. It made it too hard for her to think.

Luckily, Liam saved her from having to come up with a response. He dropped his hand back to his side.

"Wanna shoot a round?"

She frowned. "Now?"

Liam crossed the room and grabbed a couple sticks from the rack hanging on the wall. "Why not? We never get this place to ourselves. We should take advantage of it."

She accepted the pool cue from him, instinctively reaching for the blue chalk cube. Maybe a platonic game was exactly what she needed to help her get a grip. She and Liam were cutthroat competitors. The contest would be a welcome distraction. "Fine. You're on. Should we put a wager on it to make it fun? Say, twenty bucks?"

Liam shook his head. "Not interested in taking your money."

She laughed. "Doesn't matter. I didn't intend to give you any. It's you who's going to be forking over the pot when I wipe up this table with you."

He took the chalk from her with a cocky grin. "You've never beaten me. What makes you think tonight will be any different?"

She didn't confess that she'd been practicing. A lot. If there was one thing Jade hated, it was losing. After her last defeat at Liam's hands, she'd started coming in to Spurs a half hour or so before they opened to run through some drills and trick shots. Bruce—a former hustler himself—had given her some pointers as well.

"Just put the cash on the table."

"No. I want something else when I win."

Jade tilted her head, intent on continuing the trash-talking, but Liam cut her off.

"After I win, I pull down those tight jeans of yours, bend you over the table and fuck you from behind."

Jade blinked several times, then jerked away from

Liam when he reached over to close her open mouth with a strong finger on her chin.

"Is that your idea of convincing me?"

He nodded. "Yep."

"Fine," she said when she was finally able to speak. The static roaring in her ears was almost deafening. "And when I win, you..."

What the hell was she supposed to ask for? The list of sexual things she wanted to try with Liam rolled through her brain like the credits at the end of a movie—only in fast-forward. It occurred to her there were too damn many things she desired, every single act kinkier than the one before it.

Liam grasped a handful of her T-shirt and pulled her closer. "I what?"

She wasn't ready to give in just yet. "You owe me twenty dollars." Jade held out her hand and she and Liam shook on the bet.

"Deal." Liam racked the balls, then looked at her. "You want to break?"

She nodded, approaching the end of the table. Just as she bent over to line up her shot, Liam stepped behind her. His crotch rested firmly against her ass. She started to rise, but Liam's hand landed on her upper back, holding her close to the table.

"What the hell are you—?"

"Just giving you some incentive..." Liam gripped her hips tightly, rubbing his obvious erection against her. He leaned over her upper body, caging her beneath him until she could feel his hot breath. "...to lose."

The bastard swept her hair to one side before placing the sexiest kiss on her neck. Jade's pussy clenched with need. She pressed closer to his cock, wishing there weren't so many clothes between them.

Liam was fighting dirty. And winning.

If he kept this up, the game would end before it

even started. Jade forced air into her lungs, tried to beat down her desires. "You finished?" Somehow she managed to put just the right amount of boredom in her tone.

Liam chuckled. "You're not fooling me, gorgeous. But yeah, I think I'm good for now."

He stood, the air on her back suddenly cool without his presence. Jade pushed herself upright, the effort almost painful. She was hornier than she'd ever been in her life. Her body was telling her to stop fucking around, give in to what she wanted. However, her brain insisted she'd be smarter to call off the game, drive home at the speed of light and take care of business with her vibrator. Unfortunately her libido rejected the idea of another night of lackluster orgasms brought on by a lousy piece of plastic.

"Jade?"

Liam pulled her out of her thoughts. How stupid must she look standing there while her brain and body battled out exactly how she was going to get lucky tonight? Sterling was right. She was overthinking all of this. Denying herself wasn't part of her chemical makeup and yet, with Liam, she couldn't channel the impulsive, throw-caution-to-the-wind woman who'd always reigned supreme.

Why couldn't she?

Pushing her needs aside, she glared at Liam over her shoulder. "You're a cheating bastard."

His shit-eating grin was less than contrite. "Break the balls, Jade."

"Oh, I'd like to break a couple balls," she muttered as she resumed her previous position. This time, Liam left her unmolested, walking to the side to watch her shot, chuckling over her quiet threat.

Jade knocked the cue solidly, managing to place a stripe in the corner pocket. Pleased, she moved around the table and sank two more balls before missing on her third shot.

Liam was clearly surprised by her improvement. "You been practicing?"

She shrugged nonchalantly. For the next few minutes, neither of them spoke as the spirit of competition did indeed begin to overpower the sexual tension. The more things changed, the more they stayed the same. Jade felt a strange sense of comfort in that. Despite this newfound—and not entirely wanted—attraction to Liam, deep down, they were essentially the same people.

She watched him attempt a difficult shot, studying his face in his distraction. As he concentrated, she pondered how much he'd changed over the years. When she was younger, Jade had considered Liam one of the grown-ups. After all, she'd only been sixteen when they met, and he'd seemed practically ancient at twenty-one.

Now that she was twenty-four, she understood that he'd been young the night they'd met in the cemetery too. "Do you ever wonder where you'd be right now if Celia hadn't died?"

Liam froze, his gaze lifting to her face. "Where did that question come from?"

She lifted one shoulder. She didn't have a clue, but she wasn't willing to back away. Liam was an open book with her—except on the topic of Celia. No matter how many questions she'd asked about the woman over the years, Liam always found a way to dodge the conversation. "Don't you think twenty-one was sort of young to get married? I mean, I'm twenty-four and that's the last thing on my mind."

"I thought forever wasn't on your mind at all. You always say it's not for you, that you're never enduring that sort of long-term commitment."

"I'm not. And you're changing the subject. As always."

Liam stood up slowly, leaning his hip against the pool table. She stood on the opposite side. Even the distance between them wasn't enough to quench the fire she felt igniting.

"I'm not really sure how to answer that. When I proposed to Celia, there wasn't a question in my mind. I was one hundred percent certain I was doing the right thing. That I loved her and wanted to spend the rest of my life with her."

Jade hated the part of her that was actually hurt by his words. Jealousy?

"Of course, now—at the ripe old age of twenty-nine—I can't imagine ever being so sure of something. There's a confidence in youth that definitely fades with time."

"You miss her." It wasn't a question. She knew he did. Saw it in the way he disappeared inside himself whenever Celia's name was mentioned.

He nodded. "Yeah. I miss her. And I wonder from time to time where I'd be if she were still here. But those kinds of thoughts can drive you crazy if you dwell on them."

Jade understood that. Vivi had said something similar once when Jade mentioned JD, had wished that cancer hadn't taken her grandfather before she'd had the chance to meet him.

And God knew Jade had suffered too many sleepless nights as she considered her life with George in it. If he'd lived, how different would she be? Would she still be this tomboy or would she be softer? Sometimes she felt as if she'd tried to assume both the daughter and son roles, feeling sad that her father had never gotten his boy. As a result, she'd taken up fishing and shooting guns and riding motorcycles in an attempt to fill that void. Would she have chosen to do those things if George had lived?

She shook the wayward thoughts from her mind. "Did you ever play pool with Celia?"

Liam laughed and shook his head. "Nope. I never did, and I'm pretty sure Celia would have hated Spurs."

Jade reared back, shocked. While she knew the place was a dive and on any given day she wanted to punch at least a dozen of the patrons in the mouth for just being annoying in general, Jade truly loved Spurs. "Why?"

"Are you sure you want to hear about this?"

She nodded. "Yeah. If you're comfortable talking about it."

Liam didn't reply immediately and she expected him to shut her down once again. Then he released a long sigh. "Maybe it's time I did talk about her."

Liam rested the cue against a sidewall and pulled out a chair at one of the few tables in the room. He gestured for her to join him, so she did. "Celia and I were pretty young when we were together. She'd only turned twenty-one a couple of months before she died. Bars weren't part of our dating scene."

"She didn't come here on her twenty-first birthday?" Jade had been at the front door of Spurs the second Bruce unlocked it on the day she was finally deemed old enough to drink. Bruce had taken one look at her, rolled his eyes and muttered something about retiring early. Then he'd poured her a beer from the ancient keg and slid it across the bar to her, declaring it was on the house. Jade knew at that moment she'd found her place.

Liam shook his head. "Hell no, she didn't come here. She made me drive her all the way over to that dance club in Clarke called Genesis."

Jade crinkled her nose. "Why the hell would she

want to go there? That place is packed to the rafters with a bunch of tools all listening to deafening techno music and drinking those fruity daiquiris that cost a small fortune and have practically no alcohol in them."

Liam leaned back in his chair, kicking his feet out straight in front of him as he crossed them at the ankles. "Yep. That's an accurate description and that's where we went. A big group of her friends met us there. I crawled into bed after I got home that night and could still see those blinding, flashing lights when I closed my eyes. Woke up with a migraine at three a.m."

"Sounds like hell."

Liam shrugged. "It wasn't that bad. Not my favorite place, but we had a good time. Celia was more interested in going somewhere that let her get all glammed up. She spent hours doing her makeup, fixing her hair. She'd bought this sexy-as-sin leather miniskirt."

From what Jade had learned over the years about Celia Woods, she'd come to realize she and Liam's fiancée were polar opposites. Celia had attended beauty school prior to her death, intent on working in the Compton Pass hair salon, and had been Homecoming Queen during her senior year. "I bet she looked pretty."

That same odd feeling of resentment clawed its way to the surface. She was definitely jealous of a dead woman.

Liam didn't respond. Instead, he studied her face intently as Jade fought to school her features. When Liam sat up straighter, then moved his chair closer to hers, she knew she'd failed. Again.

"Celia *was* pretty. But so are you, Jade."

Jade snorted, then winced at the decidedly unattractive sound.

Liam placed his finger under her chin, forcing her to look at him. What was wrong with her? She'd never put value on physical appearance. Never needed a man to tell her she was beautiful. She liked herself and she didn't give a shit what anyone thought about her.

So why was she sitting here, dying for Liam's approval of her looks and feeling inadequate in comparison to Celia?

Liam reached between her legs and Jade felt her eyes drifting shut, hoping he'd touch her, give her some sort of relief. She'd managed to overcome her arousal during the game, but the second they'd claimed their places at the table, it had returned with a vengeance.

Unfortunately, Liam didn't touch her at all. Instead, he reached under her chair and pulled it closer to him, so close that her knees bumped against the wooden frame of his seat. Liam lifted her legs and tugged them over his outstretched thighs. Then he pulled her chair even closer.

Liam's hand returned to her face, stroking her cheek, dragging his fingers along her jaw. "I think you're one of the most beautiful women I've ever known."

His words triggered something unfamiliar—unwanted—inside her, so she reverted to character. "Flattery won't get you in my pants."

"Why haven't you ever fallen in love?"

His question pierced. "How do you know I haven't?"

He continued to caress her face. "Because I've known you since you were sixteen. I watched you push away at least half a dozen boys from school until eventually no one else bothered to come around. Since high school, you've indulged in the occasional hookups, but nothing else. So unless you're involved in some steamy, torrid online affair I don't know about, I'd say it's pretty obvious you've never given your heart to anyone."

"I'm just not interested. I've got enough bullshit to deal with in my day-to-day life without having to put up with some redneck trying to tell me what to do."

"What are you afraid of, Jade?"

She reared back and tried to put some distance between them, but Liam gripped her upper thighs, holding her legs in place on his. She didn't bother to resist. She'd discovered plenty of new things about him lately—the main one being his sheer power over her. It was heady and exciting, enticing.

"Stop trying to get away every time the conversation takes a turn you don't like."

She narrowed her eyes. "Fine. You want to talk about all this mushy-gushy shit? Why haven't you seriously dated anyone since Celia?"

"I haven't met anyone I want to date, to commit to."

"Isn't that what I just said?"

Liam shook his head. "No. It's not. I've opened myself up to that emotion before. I've let myself fall in love."

"You were a kid, Liam, playing a grown-up game. Are you even sure that's what it was? It could have just been lust."

Liam's face hardened. "I loved Celia. And I did want to marry her. I would have stood at that altar. I would have said *I do* and I would have meant it."

"Well then, you're lucky. I've never looked at anyone and seen forever. Can we call this subject closed and finish up in here? It's getting late." Jade was anxious to put some distance between them and this conversation. They were touching on subjects that made her uncomfortable. And sad.

"The game's over, Jade."

"You're forfeiting?"

"No." Liam's hands tightened on her thighs

before moving along the inside in slow, gentle rubs. Jade's chest seized when his fingers began working to free her from her jeans. She couldn't handle this. Him.

"You can't claim a prize you didn't win." Her voice gave her away, the sound too breathless. Hungry.

Liam unbuttoned her pants, lowered the zipper. "Then stop me."

Jade didn't move, offered no resistance as he lifted her ass and tugged the denim and her panties down. He slipped one of her tennis shoes off, freeing her leg from the material, while leaving them dangling from the other ankle. The entire action took mere seconds.

"How am I supposed to stop you? You're stronger than me."

He scowled. "You know better than that, Jade. You wanna stop me? Then do it. Tell me no and it all ends." Before she could say anything, he spread her legs apart even wider, his hands reaching for her pussy.

Jade hissed in a harsh breath when his finger grazed her clit. The gentle stroke wasn't enough for her and her eyes drifted closed as she waited for—silently willed—him to go on.

"Open your eyes."

She lifted her eyelids, saw that he'd leaned forward. His face was inches from hers. Her heart raced. Liam was handsome, kind, sexy, and offering her everything she wanted. Her resistance melted.

"Kiss me, Ja—"

She moved the scant distance needed, her lips on his before he finished speaking her name. Jade held him to her, her hands stroking his hair as he sucked her tongue into his mouth. His hands rested on her upper thighs. She tried to wiggle closer, hoping to encourage him to continue his exploration.

Liam's grip on her legs tightened, an unspoken

command for her to hold still. Jade forced herself to remain motionless. She tried to focus on the incredible kiss he was offering, but it was pointless. She was past the point of no return.

She pulled away. "Touch me."

Liam studied her face. "If we start this, Jade, the decision's made. No backtracking. It's going to be me, you and a bed for the next two months."

She licked her lips and tried to pull his face back to hers, hoping to evade his demand.

Liam stopped her. "Say yes. We're not taking one more step until you tell me yes."

"Liam, please."

"Jade."

His expression was resolute. He wouldn't make another move unless she agreed. Jade closed her eyes, hoping that by blinding herself to Liam's gorgeous brown eyes, his chiseled jaw, his sexy body, she'd find some way to refuse.

Shit. Who was she kidding? It really was game over.

She'd told Liam she wanted to break free of the rut she was stuck in, to go wild and she'd meant every word. Liam was offering her a dream…without strings. Clearly the heat of this summer really had gone to her head if she was seriously considering saying no.

She opened her eyes and captured Liam's gaze. Let him read the answer in her expression.

She was pleased when he smiled. "It's about time you got here."

She laughed. "I haven't quite been myself the past few weeks, have I?"

"It would appear you've turned a corner."

Jade nodded. "Oh yeah. I'm back. And ready."

"For?"

"Everything you're offering, cowboy."

Liam didn't hesitate. Didn't ask if she was certain. He knew her well enough to know she didn't mince words, didn't hem and haw once her mind was made up. And hers was.

"Tonight I'm giving you a sample. Tomorrow—the whole enchilada." He pushed two fingers inside her pussy. "Jesus, Jade."

She was wet. Hot. Hungry. He'd put her in this state weeks earlier with just a kiss, and the condition had only grown worse with each passing day. She grinned at his reverent tone. It was nice to know she hadn't been suffering alone.

Liam soon found a rhythm as he finger-fucked her. He hadn't lied about his desire to explore limits. His strokes were firm, hard, fast.

Jade gripped his shoulders in an attempt to hold on as he worked his magic. Her back arched and she tried to scoot closer to him. While his fingers were beating a furious pace, driving her to the brink too quickly, she still wanted—needed—more.

"Liam." His name fell from her lips on a gasp. He stilled for a split second before he added a third digit to the dance. His hands were large, calloused. They stretched her, taking her to the edge of discomfort, but not beyond.

His motions grew even faster, something she hadn't thought possible.

Jade dug her nails into Liam's shoulders, vaguely aware she was piercing his skin through the thin cotton of his T-shirt. It didn't matter. She couldn't let go, couldn't loosen her grip. She needed to hold on to something.

Stars flew behind her eyes and she closed them tightly. Her orgasm was imminent. It was all happening too fast. No lover had ever gotten her to the peak so quickly. Mere minutes had passed, yet Jade felt as if she was coming apart at the seams.

"Oh my God. Harder. I need it harder." Her voice sounded harsh, guttural. "Dammit." Jade struggled to breathe, fought to find air as her body began to tremble.

Liam increased his strength, his pace. She felt his gaze on her. She'd never manage to hide from him, to shield every overpowering sensation he was unleashing inside her.

"Do it, Jade. Give it to me. Let me feel you come."

She shook her head, though not in denial. It was too much, too good. She wasn't ready for it to end.

Liam misinterpreted her response. He fucked her harder, his thrusting fingers pounding rougher. "Don't fight it."

She splintered, erupted. Her back arched as she cried out loudly, a stream of obscenities flying out, one right after the other as tremor after tremor wracked her frame.

Through it all, Liam continued to stroke her, to make his hot demands. "Give me another one. More, Jade. You're so hot, you're burning my hand. Do it again."

Her body obeyed even as her mind began to reject what was happening as possible. She wasn't sure if she was having multiple orgasms or if it was just one long, never-ending moment of bliss. Geological ages passed as Liam directed her body, bending her pleasure at will, taking her further than she'd ever gone.

Finally, his hand stilled. Jade fell forward, her arms wrapped around his shoulders tightly, her face buried in the crook of his neck. She shuddered when Liam removed his fingers from her satisfyingly sore pussy. She'd pay for this night's pleasure tomorrow. Then he enclosed her in his embrace, tugging her completely onto his lap. She still straddled his legs, but their new, closer proximity allowed her to feel his rock-hard cock, buried beneath the denim of his jeans.

She sat up, besieged by guilt.

Liam tilted his face, studying hers. "Crying?"

Jade reached up to touch her cheeks, shocked to find they were indeed wet. "I—" She shook her head. "No."

Liam smiled. "It's okay, Jade. It doesn't make you weak."

"I'm not crying."

He kissed her gently, his lips surprisingly soft considering every other part of the man seemed to be chiseled from stone. His firm muscles and rough hands attested to how hard he worked for a living.

She soaked up the comfort in his tender touch for several minutes before moving. She reached for the button on his jeans, but Liam captured her wrists, tugging them away from their intended target.

She was a firm believer in fair play in the bedroom. He'd just given her one hell of an experience. Now it was her turn to return the favor.

"Not tonight, Jade. I told you. Tonight was the sample."

She frowned. "You're hard as a rock. That's gotta be painful. Let me take care of you."

He shook his head. "The first time we're together, we're going to be in a bed, not in the back room of this dive."

"It's just sex, Liam. It's not like we're on our honeymoon or something. I don't need special."

He didn't answer for a few moments and she was left to ponder the strange expression on his face. His response confused her even more.

"Yes. You do."

"You're not going to start being overly nice to me now, are you?" Despite the fact they were indulging in a racy affair, she really wanted their friendship to remain the same, complete with trash-talking and sarcasm.

Liam laughed. "Don't worry, kiddo. I have no intention of turning into some romantic sap."

"Good. Because I hate that shit." Now that the lazy haze of the aftermath of her orgasm was lifting, Jade began to feel slightly uneasy about her present state of undress.

She stood, bending over to fight with her jeans. The denim was tangled around one ankle. Liam leaned forward to help.

"You sure you're okay?" She gestured toward the erection she could still see straining against his pants.

He shrugged. "Nothing there a hand job, followed by a cold shower, can't cure."

She stepped closer. "Or my hand…and mouth…could take care of it."

Liam blew out a long, slow breath. "Fuck, Jade." He closed his eyes and he appeared to actually pray. When his gaze found hers again, his face was serene, but his eyes still betrayed his need. "I know I said that once we started, we wouldn't stop, but I want you to take tonight to think about exactly what I want, where this is going. You've had a taste, but I intend to take this a lot further. I'm not lying when I say I want your submission. You need to be sure you can handle that."

She was surprised by his determination to slow things down. Especially after he was the one so fired up to get this party started. But she was touched by his concern. It reinforced just how much she could trust Liam. He would always look out for her, have her best interest at heart. "It's your call. I mean, I'm feeling pleasantly sated. Pretty sure I'll sleep like a baby tonight."

He laughed. "Keep rubbing it in and I'll be forced

to seek revenge."

She gave him a look that let him know she wasn't worried. Once she was dressed again, Liam rose as well. Determined not to let things get weird between them, she started tidying up the room, making casual chitchat while returning their pool cues to the rack.

Liam leaned against the table with his arms crossed. It was several minutes before she realized he hadn't contributed anything to the conversation.

She turned to look at him. "What?"

"Did I hurt you?"

Jade shook her head. Though he'd taken her harder than she'd ever experienced before, the slight twinges of pain had only increased her pleasure. She wasn't sure what to make of that knowledge. Eventually she'd have to sit down and consider what that meant. But for now, she hadn't lied. Her body was relaxed, her mind too enjoyably foggy for her to worry about anything.

"Good." He reached out for her, tugging her until she was pressed tightly against his chest in what could only be called a giant bear hug. "Now for the ground rules."

She pushed away and narrowed her eyes. "You can't add guidelines to a game after it's already started."

Liam ran his hand through her hair, softly stroking it for a few seconds before wrapping a handful of the locks around his fingers and tugging. The satiation she'd felt after her orgasm faded as lust kicked in once more.

Liam tightened his grip, pulling even harder. "Ready to listen?"

Jade wanted to call him to task, but his hand in her hair was having an overwhelming effect on her libido. "Yes," she hissed.

"No one else but me, Jade."

She scowled. While she wasn't exactly innocent, she wasn't promiscuous. She didn't sleep with countless guys at the same time and Liam knew it.

"Only if you agree to the same thing."

"Goes without saying."

Jade let her annoyance creep out. "You're right. It does."

Liam didn't bother to acknowledge that his first rule pissed her off. "No more recklessness. You get the urge to do something even remotely dangerous, you come find me and I'll offer you a better alternative."

She wanted to accuse him of being a cocky asshole, but considering the orgasms he'd given her with just three fingers, she decided to let it slide. "You realize *dangerous* is a subjective term."

Liam tugged harder and forced her to look at him. He had her by at least half a foot in height, but that was never more apparent to her than now when he was towering over her and clearly not happy with her response. "We're going to use *my* interpretation of the word."

At the moment, it felt as if he was the living embodiment of a threat. However, rather than scare her, it ramped up her arousal even more. Damn him.

"Fine. I'll come find you before I do anything risky. But I'm warning you now, you better deliver on your promise or I'm not beholden to mine."

His grin turned almost wolfish as he used his free hand to pinch her ass. Hard.

She gasped, amazed by the incredible impact the pain of that simple touch provoked.

"You don't need to worry about that," he taunted, proving his point perfectly.

Jade fought to calm her racing heart. Liam may have no intention of continuing their sexual exploration tonight, but if he didn't let her go soon, she'd be forced to institute his so-called cure on herself. Only she'd be using her vibrator along with that cold shower.

"Anything else?" she asked.

"Last one. If you do anything that I consider unsafe, I have the right to punish you."

Feminism reared its head. "No. You don't."

Liam slapped her ass this time, the action sending sparks of electricity straight to her pussy. If this was what he meant by a penalty, she needed to shut the hell up and agree.

"That's non-negotiable, Jade."

Jade's ability to think clearly faded, obliterated by the sensual needs Liam awakened inside her.

"Whatever. Okay. Correct me. However you want to." The thought of Liam taking her over his knees and spanking her bare ass flashed before her eyes.

Liam must've recognized the desire lacing her tone as she agreed to his final rule. "Don't go inviting trouble. I promise you. You won't enjoy my discipline."

As he spoke, he released her, taking a step away. She didn't like the distance, so she sought to close it, reaching for the button of his jeans. The orgasm she'd experienced earlier was ancient history, her body suddenly demanding more.

Liam halted her, the grin on his face one she instantly mistrusted.

"I want you," she insisted.

Liam turned away from her, walking toward the bar. Glancing over his shoulder, he winked. "Revenge is a bitch."

Chapter Five

Liam rubbed his neck as he drove down the narrow lane that would take him home. Nearly a week had passed since he and Jade had *supposedly* begun their summer fling. Seven days and he'd yet to have sex with the woman. Not that they hadn't tried. Unfortunately, circumstances conspired against them. He'd been out of town earlier in the week, meeting with a team of rodeo organizers, bidding to outfit several large state events. It had been a successful trip, but it had kept him away from home and Jade for four days.

Once he'd returned, Liam found Jade laid up in bed with a nasty head cold. He had taken her some soup and watched a couple movies with her, but she'd refused to even kiss him for fear of giving him her illness.

Tonight, she was better, but it was Bruce who'd been under the weather. Her boss had asked Liam to stick around again to help Jade close, and Liam had finally spied an opportunity to take things to the next level. Until they'd found Chuckie Dupont passed out in the bathroom. It had fallen to Liam to drive the dumbass home, while Jade assured him she could finish things at the bar.

Liam tried to decide if he should say to hell with

it and take the turn-off to Compass Ranch. He had made a mistake when laying out the ground rules. Liam had put the decision of *when* they hooked up in Jade's hands, telling her to seek him out whenever she felt the urge to do something crazy.

That miscalculation was costing him. For a week, he'd walked around with a perpetual hard-on, unable to think of anything except pulling Jade Compton under him and fucking her nonstop until the end of August.

Brake lights in the distance caught his attention, and he slowed down. While the road led to quite a few homes in the area, it was unusual for him to come across someone out so late. His heart began to pound when he saw Jade's motorcycle along the side of the road. In front of it, he spotted a car wrapped around a large oak tree.

Liam pulled up behind Jade's bike and parked. He quickly dialed 911 and told the operator to send an ambulance to Redbud Lane.

Rushing from the truck, he spotted Jade at the driver's side door, struggling to pull a man from the vehicle. He hadn't taken two steps toward her before he was assaulted by the smell of gas. Then he noticed the flames flickering under the hood.

Jesus.

He ran toward Jade, yelling for her to get away. She didn't acknowledge him. Instead she continued to tug at the unconscious man, her frantic actions attesting to the fact that she knew exactly what kind of danger she was courting.

When he reached her, he tried to pull her to safety, but she fought him.

"Jade. Run. The car could explode."

She shook her head, refusing to release the man. "It's Bruce. Help me." Her voice was filled with terror, panic.

"I'll get him. Get away from here!"

"No."

"Dammit, Jade! I'm not fucking around. Move. Now!"

"Help me or get out of my way, Liam! I'm not leaving until he's safe." While Jade and her boss constantly yelled and screamed and cursed at each other, Liam knew she loved Bruce like he was family. She wouldn't leave his side until he was well clear of the burning vehicle.

"Slide over. Let me get a grip on him." Bruce was no small man, but between the two of them, they managed to drag him out of the driver's seat seconds before the fire spread from under the hood, flames engulfing the dashboard and the mangled steering wheel.

Time wasn't on their side. They grasped Bruce under his arms, straining to pull the man across the road, away from the danger, the imminent explosion. They'd just reached the other side when Liam heard a series of loud pops.

He laid Bruce on the ground, then grabbed Jade's head and pushed her low as well. "Get down!"

Together they covered Bruce's body with theirs as the blaze reached the gas tank. A deafening boom followed by an intense wall of heat hit Liam like a freight train. Jade trembled beneath him as he sought to shelter her. For several moments, neither of them moved as huge, leaping flames traveled along the trunk of the tree, consuming it. A sharp crack pierced the night as one of the large, lower branches gave way and fell.

While the fire continued to burn, the flaring plumes of orange and yellow grew smaller. Like the powerful outburst experienced when starter fluid is thrown on a lit campfire, the blaze died down once its fuel burned out.

Jade was the first to rise. Her face was white as a sheet and tear-stained. Liam realized exactly how terrified she'd been. He could relate. His hands were shaking and his heart was pounding so hard it felt as if it would burst right out of his chest. He reached over to cup her face.

"You okay?"

She nodded, though her eyes were wide. Liam briefly wondered if she was going into shock. Then, in typical Jade fashion, she powered through the fear more quickly than he was going to be able to. She glanced down at Bruce, placing her fingers against her boss's carotid artery, checking his pulse. Liam looked for injuries, but the air bag appeared to have done its job. Apart from a wicked red mark on his right cheek and what was definitely going to be a black eye, Liam couldn't see any cuts or scratches that looked too serious. His main concern was the fact the man was still unconscious.

"Bruce." Jade lightly shook the man's shoulders. "Bruce. Wake up. Can you hear me?"

Bruce moaned, his eyelids fluttering a bit before they closed once more.

A siren sounded in the distance. Jade looked toward the road.

"I called 911 as soon as I came upon the accident," he explained.

Jade smiled. "Good thinking. The second I saw Bruce's car, I hopped off my bike and ran to him. Never occurred to me to phone anyone."

Her admission bothered Liam. While it wasn't unusual for Jade to leap in to situations—breaking up fights at the bar, answering fire alarms and the like—she never remembered to ask for help, even if she needed it.

Jade glanced at the burning vehicle. "Fuck."

Liam looked over his shoulder to see what had upset her. "Oh damn, kiddo. I'm sorry." The tree branch that had broken during the fire had fallen onto her motorcycle, doing more than its fair share of damage. Fortunately for him, only a few smaller limbs had reached his pickup truck. While the paint was probably scratched, his vehicle was still drive-able. The same wasn't true for Jade's bike.

Jade blew out a long, annoyed breath, but she didn't complain. Instead, she gazed down at Bruce again. "It's okay. The motorcycle can be fixed. If that's the worst thing that happens tonight…" Her words faded away, her voice breaking.

She was clearly worried about Bruce.

"He'll be okay, Jade."

She nodded, blinking back tears, refusing to let them fall.

"Did you see the accident?" Liam asked.

Jade shook her head. "No. Bruce left about a half hour before us, remember?" She shuddered lightly and Liam knew she was thinking about how close her boss had come to losing his life. That was the one thought that kept beating a steady rhythm in his mind, but the name of the victim was different for him.

Jade could have died.

A police car parked near them, Sawyer stepping out. The sheriff studied the burning vehicle for only a second as he ran toward them.

Jade rose quickly as her father approached, calling out her name. "Jade!"

"I'm fine, Dad." Her calmly spoken reassurance was belied by her actions. Though she wasn't usually overly affectionate, Liam watched as she accepted her father's strong embrace, clinging to him, sniffling against his shirt.

"What happened?" Sawyer asked, looking at Liam, refusing to release Jade.

"Bruce was in an accident. We're not sure what caused it. Jade got here first, then I happened along."

Jade took a small step back, looking up at her dad's face. "We pulled him out. Then a few minutes later, it caught fire and exploded."

Liam narrowed his eyes at Jade's false interpretation of events. She didn't bother to look his way. Instead, she kept her eyes steadfastly directed at her father.

"Jesus," Sawyer muttered, pulling Jade back into his arms. "You could have been hurt."

She could have been killed. Liam didn't speak the thought aloud. Her father was shaken up enough.

Another siren and more flashing lights approached. The ambulance stopped next to Sawyer's patrol car and soon, three EMTs surrounded Bruce as the firefighters arrived with the tanker, working to douse the flames that had already started to wane. It would have burned out on its own, but given the lack of rain and dry summer they'd had, Liam knew they were smart to douse the area with water in order to prevent a potential flare-up or brushfire.

Sawyer looked at Jade's mangled motorcycle. "I'll call Rex and have him come pick up your bike. He can take it back to the shop."

"Thanks," Jade answered distractedly. Her attention was on the EMTs who had put Bruce on a gurney and were loading him into the rescue squad.

Liam placed a hand on her shoulder. "Come on, kiddo. I'll give you a lift to the hospital. We can wait to see what the doctor says and then I'll take you home."

She looked at Liam appreciatively. "Really? You sure you don't mind?"

He shook his head. There was no way he was

letting her out of his sight for a while. He was still too shaken up by all the *what ifs*. There were a lot of uneasy feelings churning in his gut. Until he figured out how to deal with them, he was sticking to her like glue.

"Thanks, Liam." Sawyer slapped him on the shoulder. "I really need to hang out here a little longer to record the scene, then write my report. I'll stop by Circle H some time tomorrow to get a statement from you."

Liam nodded. "That's fine."

Sawyer reached for Jade again and she stepped into his arms. "I really am okay, Dad." Her voice sounded exasperated, though Liam didn't think she minded her father's hug as much as she pretended.

Sawyer placed a kiss to the top of her head. "Yeah. I know. Humor me."

They held on to each other for a few more seconds before pulling apart. "I'll stop by your cabin tomorrow to check on you. And you might want to tidy up a bit because you know your mom, grandma and all the aunts will be around to make sure you're okay."

She rolled her eyes. "Seriously? Do you have to tell them about this?"

Sawyer chuckled. "I won't have to say a word. There are at least half a dozen people here, all ready to share the tale. I guarantee you there won't be a single person in Compton Pass who won't know all the details about this accident by midday tomorrow."

Jade sighed. "Shit."

Sawyer walked toward the wrecked car as Liam grasped Jade's hand and led her to his pickup. They rode to the hospital in silence, both of them coming down hard from the adrenaline rush provoked by their brush with near-death.

Liam was assaulted by the memory of the night the state patrolman had knocked on the door to Celia's parents' house. He'd driven over to see them after Mrs. Woods called to ask if Celia had been in touch with him. She was late getting back from Denver and wasn't answering her phone. Liam had been the one to answer the door when they saw the police car pull into the driveway. He'd listened calmly as the policeman explained about the accident, told them how there was nothing Celia could have done, how she hadn't suffered.

The same numbness Liam had felt that night settled in. He couldn't go through that again. He wouldn't. Suddenly the game he'd been playing with Jade felt foolish. Wrong.

They sat in the hospital waiting room for nearly an hour, neither of them speaking, before the doctor appeared.

Jade rose as he approached. "Is Bruce okay?"

The doctor nodded. "He'll be fine, but we're keeping him here to run a few more tests. He listed you as his next of kin." Bruce was a confirmed bachelor with no wife, no kids and no relatives—his parents long since dead and his only estranged sister living somewhere on the East Coast. Dr. Henderson understood Jade was as close as he was going to get to family, so he'd likely gotten Bruce's permission to share information with her.

"What's wrong with him?"

Dr. Henderson shrugged. "Several things. The one that concerns me the most right now is his blood pressure. It's sky-high, and we're working on bringing it down. He's also got a blockage in his heart that may require a stent, and his ulcer is back."

"He's had one before?"

The doctor gave her a weary smile. "Bruce had a nasty ulcer a few years ago. I treated it, suggested he alter his diet. I don't think I have to tell you he's pretty set in his ways and not generally open to change."

Jade released a loud *ha*. "He's stubborn as a mule. Stupid, infuriating asshole. I told him it was something serious a week ago."

Liam lightly laid his hand on the small of Jade's back, hoping to calm her down. Her fear had initially turned to worry, but now annoyance and frustration were kicking in. "He was really out of it after the accident, Doc. Ulcers don't do that, do they?"

Dr. Henderson rubbed the back of his neck. "No. That was due to the high blood pressure. I can only assume he lost consciousness while he was driving. He's lucky you were both there and able to get him help so quickly."

"Can I see him?" Jade asked.

"He's asleep right now. I'd suggest that you go on home and get some rest, Jade, then come back in the morning. If he responds well to the medication we've put him on, he may be able to leave the hospital as early as the day after tomorrow."

The doctor's words clearly went a long way toward setting Jade's mind at ease. "Thanks." Exhaustion was written on her face, in her posture. Time for bed.

Liam led Jade back to his truck. She was silent for most of the trip. In fact, Liam suspected she'd fallen asleep for a few minutes. Unfortunately, she woke up too soon.

"You missed the turn off to Compass Ranch."

Liam didn't respond. He'd driven by it on purpose. He'd had no intention of taking her to her house.

"Liam? Are you awake? Are you paying attention?"

"I know where we're going, Jade."

She narrowed her eyes. "Turn around."

"No."

Jade released a loud, frustrated breath. "Look, in case you forgot the rules, I'm supposed to come find you. I'm tired and not in the mood. Now take me home."

"There was more than one ground rule."

Jade scowled. "I haven't slept with anyone else."

He grinned. She was being purposely obtuse. "Try again."

"You're not seriously planning to punish me for saving someone's life."

That wasn't his plan, but he couldn't let go of the fact she'd put her own life at serious risk tonight. His head was pounding, his chest tight, the tension building. Every man had a breaking point, and whether Jade realized it or not, he'd hit his.

He'd promised her a summer fling and he intended to follow through on that. But he wasn't in this for the short-term. He never had been. And while he hadn't clued Jade in to his true intentions yet, the ache in his gut that had been there all evening as he considered how close he'd come to losing her, told him he was probably about to botch things up.

It didn't matter. His mother warned him his need to control things beyond his power was going to come back to bite him in the ass. Looked like that day had arrived.

He turned down the dirt road that led to his ranch, not bothering to reply to Jade.

In typical fashion, her temper flared hot and fast. "Goddammit, Liam Harrison. You turn this fucking truck around and drive me to Compass Ranch or so help me, I'll kick your ass."

Liam had learned a long time ago that the quickest way to get under Jade's skin was to ignore her when she was in the midst of a temper tantrum. For some reason, her anger pleased him. It matched his own right now, put them on equal ground. His blood was boiling.

Liam was furious.

At her. Bruce. Life. Fate. All of it.

Once he reached the house, he turned off the truck.

Jade turned to face him. "I'm not getting out."

He grinned. "Of course you are."

She glared at him, daggers flying. "If you're trying to piss me off, you're doing a great job."

Liam climbed out, walking around the hood until he was at her door. Jade sat with her arms crossed, staring toward the house with a look on her face that promised she would make him pay if he touched her.

Liam loved a good dare. He opened the door and reached for her seat belt. She tried to shove his arm away, but he unbuckled her, then grasped her waist, tugging her out of the vehicle easily.

Jade exploded with fury, kicking and punching him in her attempts to break free. She put up a good fight, but Liam didn't release her until she was on her feet, standing next to the passenger door. Then he pushed her against it, caging her in.

She pushed, shoved, tried dodging under his arms, but Liam managed to keep her trapped. Finally, she stilled, her breathing labored, her face flushed.

"What do you want?" she asked, offering as much of a surrender as he'd likely get from her tonight.

Too fucking much. Liam should have taken her home. Spent the night trying to get his raging emotions under control.

It was too late for common sense now. Instead, he let all the irrational fears that had consumed him for the past couple of hours surface. "I told you to get away from that car. You could have been killed."

Jade frowned. "I couldn't leave Bruce there."

"I know that, Jade. Believe me, I fucking get it. It still doesn't help."

"What do you want me to say? I'm sorry? Because I'm not."

He shook his head. "I don't want an apology." His gaze drifted lower. Her breathing was rapid, causing her chest to rise and fall, drawing his attention to her breasts. Before he could consider his actions, he lifted his hand, cupped her plump flesh and squeezed. Hard.

Jade's head fell back and a soft moan escaped.

Liam's weak grip on his emotions slipped. He took a step away from her, grasping her hand and pulling her toward his house. Jade struggled briefly, obviously surprised by his quick moves.

"Liam, wait."

"No."

Jade dug in her heels as they reached the front porch, but Liam wouldn't be denied. Not now. Not ever.

Turning, he hoisted her over his shoulder and carried her into the house. He glanced up the stairs that would take them to his bedroom, then decided that was too far away. He stepped into the living room instead, not stopping until they reached the couch where he set her down.

Jade bounced back up instantly, but Liam pushed her onto the cushions, keeping her in place with a strong hand on her shoulder.

"Holy fuck. Do you have some sort of death wish or what?" Jade's fury returned in spades.

He knelt in front of her, moving his hands to her legs. Parting them, he kept a firm grip on her upper thighs.

"I almost lost you tonight." They were the only words he could think to say, the same painful thought that had permeated his consciousness until nothing else remained.

"Wrong. You never had me."

She didn't understand. Couldn't grasp the terror he'd felt when he'd seen her standing beside that burning car. Somehow he'd have to make her comprehend.

"Fearless," he said.

"What?"

"Your safe word. It's Fearless. If you get scared or the pain is too much and you want me to stop, say that word and I will. But, please, Jade, don't use it lightly." He studied her face, watching as she processed it all. "Say it. Let me hear you say it."

"Fearless," she whispered.

That softly spoken word was all he needed. It set Liam free. Rising, he pulled her up, claiming her spot on the couch. Before she could react to his fast movements, he tugged her facedown over his lap.

"What the hell are you doing?" Jade tried to push away, but Liam pressed her head lower, so close to the floor her hair touched the hardwood.

He lifted his hand and brought it down roughly against her ass. While the jeans muted the blow, the shock of his spanking caused Jade to still. She didn't say the safe word or fight him, so he took it as permission to continue. He slapped her half a dozen times more, building the intensity as he struck the same spot over and over.

Jade remained motionless through only the first couple smacks, then she began to struggle. At first, Liam thought she was trying to escape his blows.

"Jade?"

She shook her head, remaining silent, and soon it

became obvious she was moving toward his hand, trying to add even more fuel to the fire. She latched on to his lower leg for support, her grip tight as a vise.

She wanted more. So did he.

He lifted her, directed her to her feet, despite Jade's protestations.

"Take off your pants," he commanded.

Jade's flushed face, her hungry eyes, her tight nipples told him all he needed to know, as she reached for the button on her jeans.

Liam rose, shoving her hands away. She was going too slowly. His cock was thick and hard, throbbing in the confinement of his own tight denim. He didn't dare free it or he'd never finish what he'd started.

For much of his younger years, he'd resisted the part of him that craved rough sex. Celia had been a virgin when they'd first made love. She preferred to be cuddled, caressed, kissed. Liam had given her that because he adored her. If being her husband meant locking away certain desires, he'd do it, and willingly. After her death, he slowly began to let the darker pleasures he yearned for emerge.

However, Compton Pass was a small town. People talked. So he'd only indulged in BDSM games while on the road on business trips. Until now. There was no power on earth that could stop him from showing Jade the real Liam.

As he tugged her jeans and panties down, Jade toed off her sandals. Within seconds, he'd returned them to their previous positions, Liam sitting on the couch, Jade sprawled out over his lap. Her ass was flushed a light pink from his earlier spanking. It wasn't enough. He longed to paint it red, to set the sensitive skin on fire.

"Please." Jade squirmed on his lap, so he placed a

sharp slap to her upper thigh.

Then Liam stroked between her legs, along the opening to her sex. Jade gasped when he pressed on her clit. She was drenched, her arousal coating his fingers. All of his suspicions were confirmed in an instant. Not only did Jade enjoy his rough touch, it turned her on.

"Liam," she said, his name escaping on a breathless sigh.

Hearing her voice caused something to twist inside. His head reeled from it. The night had tumbled down like one long string of dominos, each tile that fell taking a hundred more out until Liam wasn't sure what was left. All he knew was he had to find some way to make Jade Compton understand she was going to be a hell of a lot more than a summer fling.

She was going to be his wife, his partner on the ranch and the mother of his children.

But for now…his hesitance confused her.

Jade twisted, looking over her shoulder at him. "I trust you."

He grinned, thrilled by her words. He stroked her ass gently. The words "I love you" floated across his brain, but he didn't speak them aloud. She wasn't ready for that.

He had two months to wrap his Compass girl up in ropes so tight she wouldn't be able to escape. He'd bind her to him not only with friendship, but with craving, need, and, God willing, love.

"Close your eyes, Jade."

She blinked twice before her eyelids lowered, then she turned around until she faced the floor once more.

Liam lifted his hand and lowered it on her ass and upper thighs. He didn't hold back, didn't bother to shield his strength. He knew her better than anyone— knew her limits as well as her longing to go wild, to take things just to the edge, and then, maybe, even a bit further. He would be the only man to give her this, to keep her safe while setting her free. It was the only way he'd ever hold her and claim her heart.

Jade wouldn't—no, she couldn't—live her life in the conventional way. She'd feel stifled, trapped in a world where she followed the rules associated with being a woman, a wife, a mother. Hell, he didn't want her to fit those molds.

He loved her courage, her bravery, her recklessness, her foul mouth and her loud, brash laughter. Liam continued to spank her as so many realizations assaulted him.

Love. Forever. Marriage.

Jade. Jade. Jade.

She squeezed his leg roughly as she groaned—the sound a perfect blend of agony and indulgence.

"God, Liam." Her voice was thick with unshed tears and demand. "Please make me feel this. Make me feel *something*. I'm so tired of being numb."

He missed a stroke, then recognized the truth behind her admission. Jade had admitted to being restless, but now he knew it was more than that. She'd always seemed like the square peg in the round hole. That should have been evident to him from the start.

Hadn't he met her in a cemetery, kneeling at her dead brother's grave? How many years had Jade smothered her own flame out of some misplaced feelings of guilt over being the sibling who lived?

Her ass and legs were bright red, yet she still pushed toward him, silently begging for more. Jade wanted to come alive. So did he.

He'd carried around more than his own fair share of blame following Celia's accident. He should have driven her to the city, should have insisted on going with her rather than caving to her admonition about the danger of him seeing her in her wedding dress.

Enough. The past was dead and buried.

It was time he and Jade started living in the present. Made some strides toward the future.

His hand stilled, covering her ass. Jade's breathing was loud, labored, dotted with the occasional hitch that told him she was on the verge of crying.

Or coming.

Or both.

He lifted her, pushing her to her back on the couch. Jade spread her legs and lifted her arms in invitation.

"I need you," she whispered.

Liam kicked off his shoes and shed his jeans in record time. He didn't bother to remove his shirt or hers. Next time they'd manage to make it to the bed, to get naked.

This time…

He knelt between her spread thighs, holding himself over her as he pressed his cock to her opening. She was soaked, the juices of her arousal allowing the head of his dick to slide in easily.

Neither of them looked away, their gazes connected as he slowly drove deeper into her tight, hot pussy. Once he was fully seated, he paused, studying her face.

Jade smiled, the expression completely her. Mischievous, naughty, daring. "You could at least offer to wear a condom."

"You've been on birth control since you were seventeen."

She rolled her eyes. "I'm not sure how I feel about sleeping with someone who knows all my secrets."

He kissed her. Couldn't resist. Jade stiffened for the briefest of moments, but it was enough for Liam to know she wasn't finished fighting this.

Them.

Regardless of his intentions, his battle to win her heart was only just beginning. He pulled away and looked at her.

Jade wrapped her legs more tightly around his waist, lifting her hips in an attempt to take control of the situation. She didn't want the romance. She wanted the fucking.

Too bad for her. She was getting both.

"Don't stop now," she demanded.

He cupped the sides of her head in his palms, letting her know without words that he held the upper hand. Bending forward, he kissed her again. Softly.

Jade stilled for a split second before opening her lips, urging him to deepen the kiss. He didn't take the bait. Instead, he kept his touches gentle.

It threw her off-guard.

"Liam," she whispered after several minutes. "Fuck me."

Rather than respond, he twisted his fingers in her hair, tugging at the long blonde tresses until her back arched.

"Yes," she hissed.

"I'm changing the rules again." He punctuated his words with a rougher pull.

Jade's chest rose and fell rapidly, the action pressing her breasts against him in a way that drove him crazy. His cock twitched, but he forced himself to remain motionless within her.

"What do you mean?"

"Sex isn't going to be on your terms only. If I want you, I'm coming to find you."

She tried to shake her head, to refuse him, but he tightened his grip on her hair. She gasped. Jade tried to lift her hips, seeking to control the situation again. Liam dropped lower, pushed more of his weight against her in order to hold her still on the cushions.

"Goddammit, Liam. I don't want to talk about this right now. Fucking move or get out of me."

He tilted his head to her neck, placing an openmouthed kiss on her soft skin before sinking his teeth in, marking her.

Her pussy muscles clenched against his cock. Liam held firm, resolute. For several minutes, he alternated between sucking, biting, licking the soft skin of her neck. No doubt she'd spend a few days trying to cover up the visual reminder he was giving her of this night.

"If you give me a hickey, I'm going to kill you."

He lifted his head and grinned. "Too late."

She slapped her hand over the spot. "You jackass. What are we? Fifteen?"

"We're going to have sex whenever or wherever we choose, Jade. I'll tie you up, spank that sexy ass of yours, fuck you as hard as you want, but you'll stop trying to call the shots."

She hesitated only a moment before nodding. "Fine. Now can we cut the conversation and get to the good stuff?"

He'd started with the easy demands. There was still one more and it would be a miracle if he got her to agree, but it was the only thing he truly wanted.

"In a minute. I want you to stay here for the next two months."

"Fuck off." Jade tried to shove him away from her, but he didn't budge, didn't give way. "Are you insane? No way. No deal."

She was resolute that the two of them were incompatible for anything long-term and serious. Liam was determined to prove her wrong.

Jade continued to push against his shoulders in an

attempt to escape. He grasped her wrists, pressing them firmly to the couch, next to her head. He lifted his hips and thrust in powerfully.

Jade's head flew back. "God," she cried. "Yes."

He gave her three more rough shoves, his cock pounding inside her until she stopped trying to flee. Her legs tightened around his waist, urging him to continue. He pressed in once more, deeper this time and with more strength than he'd ever let loose with a woman.

He bit her shoulder as he continued to fuck her hard. Then he soothed the spot with his tongue, his lips. "Move in."

Jade pressed her eyes closed tightly, but when she refused him again, the word "n-no" came softer and with a stutter as he beat a relentless rhythm inside her body.

Releasing her hands, he reached lower, cupping the sore flesh of her ass in his palms. Her skin was still hot to the touch. He squeezed, reminding her of his rough spanking, making sure she understood exactly what he was offering.

"Liam!" Her cries of pleasure were as loud as her laughter. Jade was a study in contradictions. In so many ways, she held back nothing, giving a hundred percent of herself. In her work, in sex, or while riding her horse or her motorcycle, she set herself free completely. However, when it came to her heart, she refused to offer even the slightest peek inside, locking it away tightly.

She was close to the edge. Liam needed to stake his claim now or he'd lose this game for good. Come morning if he hadn't secured her agreement, she'd retreat. "Stay with me, Jade."

She didn't reply, didn't bother to shake her head. Liam wasn't sure she'd even heard him.

He stilled once more, then nipped her earlobe,

forcing her to look at him.

"Please," she whispered. The desolate sound was almost his undoing. She needed her release, physically, but also emotionally. She was afraid.

It didn't matter. He couldn't give in.

"Two months, Jade. That's all I'm asking for." *For now.*

She licked her lips, then nodded slowly. "Fine. Okay. But that's all. No more new rules."

He was careful to school his features, to hide the smile threatening to consume his face. Jade would interpret it as gloating and it would piss her off.

He didn't bother to tell her he didn't need anything else. He kissed her roughly, giving her the strong, overpowering touches she'd been seeking earlier.

Then he resumed his pace, pounding deeper and harder into her. His motions were driven by elation, tinged with desperation.

He had two months to overcome Jade's fears, to prove to her he was the only man for her. To win her heart.

Jade dug her nails into his shoulders as she cried out with her release. Her pussy clamped down on his cock so deliciously, Liam didn't bother to hold back. They had time now.

He called out her name as he came, filling her, as she arched against him, accepting every drop. Once their breathing had returned to normal, he twisted them on the couch so that she lay against his chest.

Her breathing grew slower, deeper as she fell asleep. Liam tightened his grip, holding her close, relishing the beginning of the rest of his life.

Chapter Six

Liam awoke to the sound of banging. He squinted as the bright sunlight assaulted his eyes. Then he felt the pins and needles attacking his left arm. Glancing down, he realized the source of his pain. Jade was sound asleep, nestled in his hold. He savored how good it felt to have her there.

While last night had been an eye-opening experience, Liam didn't pretend things were going to be smooth-sailing from this point on. Jade wasn't finished resisting him yet.

They'd passed out on the couch briefly, but Jade had awoken him a few hours earlier, tugging off her shirt and his as she rode him slowly, leisurely. Her actions had been an attempt on her part to seize some of the control he'd claimed. And he'd let her. Hell, there was nothing hotter than a sexy cowgirl riding his cock. He might prefer the dominant role most of the time, but he also didn't look a gift horse in the mouth. The sight of Jade's tits bouncing as she pressed up and down on his dick was a vision he intended to carry with him for the rest of his life.

The pounding continued. Someone was at the door. Liam carefully lifted Jade so he could free his arm, then he tried to stand without jarring her too much.

His foreman was probably wondering where the hell he was. Liam never overslept, never failed to show up at the stable before everyone else.

Liam fastened his jeans but didn't bother to tug on his T-shirt. He wasn't going to work this morning. Once he gave his foreman instructions, he'd wake Jade and the two of them would move their physical explorations upstairs to his bedroom.

Walking to the foyer, he opened the door, but the apology for his tardiness died on his lips when he spotted Sawyer Compton on the threshold. "Sheriff."

"Jade never made it home last night."

He'd forgotten about Sawyer's plans to question them both in regards to Bruce's car accident. Liam rubbed his jaw, wondering how he could get out of this predicament with most of his body parts intact. Sawyer Compton had a reputation for being the world's most overprotective father, next to his brother Silas. Not that Liam blamed him. Jade was his only daughter and given her penchant for landing into trouble, he could understand Sawyer's need to keep a close eye on her.

"I know."

Sawyer opened the screen door and pushed his way into the house, past Liam. "Is she here?"

"Yeah." Liam didn't bother to deny a truth they both knew.

Of course, Jade chose that moment to reveal herself. "I'm trying to sleep, Clayton. You and Wyatt go somewhere else to talk," she demanded from the living room. Liam could tell from her drowsy voice she was still asleep and didn't have a clue who she was admonishing. Apparently she thought she was at home in her own cabin with her cousins and their boyfriends.

Sawyer walked toward the living room, straight to the couch where Jade lay, only partially covered by the blanket he'd pulled over them last night. She was on her stomach, eyes closed, hands thrown over her head. The blanket rode high enough to reveal evidence of his handprints of her thighs and there was no denying she was completely naked beneath it.

Liam winced when he spotted faint red marks on her neck and shoulder where he'd bitten her. He walked over to adjust the blanket, covering her better, even though it was too late. Jade's dad had gotten an eyeful. Liam didn't want to know what the sheriff was thinking, but he suspected it began and ended with his own very painful death.

Sawyer's jaw tensed as he turned his angry gaze on Liam. "Is there something you want to tell me, Liam?"

Jade jerked awake at the sound of her father's voice, lifting her head slightly from the pillow. She blinked against the bright sunlight, took in his appearance and her father's, then dropped her head down once more.

"Shit," she muttered. "What time is it?"

Sawyer glanced at the clock on the mantel. "Eleven a.m."

"Why are you here so early?"

Sawyer put his hands on his hips, the position reminding Liam of one he'd seen Jade assume anytime she was pissed off. "Eleven is early?"

"I got off work at one thirty. Pulled Bruce out of a burning car at two. Sat in the emergency room until three. Dealt with this asshole—" she gestured at Liam "—until six. So yeah, Dad. To answer your question, eleven is early."

Sawyer scowled. "Get dressed, Jade. I'll drive you home."

Liam stepped closer to the couch. His life was already in danger, he might as well go for broke. If Jade escaped now, Liam would have to fight like the devil to get her back. He suffered no illusions that her agreement to move in with him for the next two months was set in stone yet. There was work left to do.

"I'll take her to Compass Ranch. Later." And he'd remain there while she packed her stuff, then he'd bring her right back here.

Sawyer's eyes darkened, and Liam cursed his wayward tongue. Probably not smart to piss off a man with a gun. Sawyer rarely wore a real police uniform, opting for jeans and a polo shirt with a small logo of Compton Pass Sheriff's Department on the right-hand side. But he never failed to include the gun belt.

Jade groaned. "Just let me sleep a little while longer, Dad. Liam can drive me home in an hour or so. Okay?"

Sawyer didn't reply immediately. His face told Liam he wasn't *okay* with anything that was going on.

Finally, he nodded. "Fine, Jade." Sawyer started for the front door before turning to catch Liam's eye. He tilted his head, indicating he expected Liam to follow.

While he didn't believe the sheriff would assault him on his own property, Liam wasn't willing to bet the farm on that.

The Compton men were infamous for their defending natures. If anyone threatened their family, they stepped in and took care of it.

Liam may have been twenty years younger, but he didn't harbor any misapprehensions that Sawyer couldn't kick his ass if he was pissed off enough.

Liam glanced at the couch. Jade's eyes had drifted closed once more. She was oblivious to the fact her father hadn't left peacefully. Good. He didn't want her as a witness if Sawyer did decide to clean his clock.

Liam followed Sawyer.

"Are you dating my daughter?" Sawyer asked the

second the porch door closed behind him.

Liam rubbed his unshaven jaw and tried to decide what the best—safest—answer was. He suspected Sawyer was hoping he'd say yes because it would somehow alleviate the pain associated with finding Jade naked on his couch. Put a somewhat more respectable spin on it...if that was possible. However, Liam knew Jade well enough to know she'd correct anyone who tried to call him her boyfriend. He needed to play his cards right, but he wasn't sure which Compton was the safer one to piss off—Jade or her father.

Telling the sheriff what he was allowing Jade to believe, that this was just a summer fling, that he was merely fucking Sawyer's daughter because he got a hard-on every time she was within fifty feet of him, was a route fraught with peril and sure death. Unfortunately, it was probably the better way to go if he hoped to succeed in winning Jade's heart.

"Not exactly."

"Did you put those marks on her neck? Her legs?"

Liam swallowed hard, his throat constricting. There was no way in hell he could explain to Sawyer how much Jade had enjoyed his rough claiming, but one look at Sawyer's face told him it was pointless to deny something so obvious. "Yeah. I did."

"If you were any other man in town, I'd fucking kill you for that."

Liam frowned, confused. Why was he getting a bye?

"But I know you. I've watched you with my daughter. You'd never hurt Jade."

Liam nodded. "You're right. I wouldn't."

"You two have been friends for years and I'll bet a hundred dollars you've never crossed that line before. So what's changed? Why now?"

Liam didn't bother to lie. "It wasn't minutes."

Sawyer's brow crinkled. "What?"

"The car didn't explode minutes after we pulled Bruce out. It was only seconds."

Sawyer's face went white. "What the fuck are you saying?"

"When I got to the accident, Jade was already at the driver's side door, trying to get Bruce out. How that wisp of a woman thought she was going to pull a man who's nearly twice her size away from a burning vehicle, I'll never know, but she was sure as hell trying. I smelled the gas as soon as I got out of my truck."

"Why didn't you get her away?" Sawyer's tone was pure fury.

"You think I didn't try? Jesus, Sawyer. I yelled, I cussed, I tried to drag her back. It didn't matter. She wasn't going anywhere without Bruce. So I grabbed one side of him, she got the other and somehow we got Bruce across the street just before the car exploded."

Sawyer put his hands on the railing of the porch, and for a second, Liam thought the man was using them to hold him upright. "Mother of God. She could've been killed."

There had been an ache in Liam's gut ever since he'd come upon the accident. He'd spent last night trying to reconcile himself to what Sawyer had just learned. They'd come damn close to losing her. If Liam hadn't arrived when he had, there wasn't a doubt in his mind that Jade would never have left her beloved boss's side. She would have died with him.

"I can't stop replaying it in my mind."

Sawyer looked at Liam, his gaze filled with an understanding that was difficult for Liam to acknowledge. "So you brought her back here. And things changed."

Liam nodded.

"I see."

For the first time, Liam noticed something he'd never seen before in the sheriff's posture, his expression, some indefinable vein of strength that marked them as kindred spirits. Maybe he would escape this conversation unscathed after all.

"She cares about you, Liam. You've always been a good friend to her. I'm not sure exactly what's going on between you and Jade. Leah would tell me it's none of my damn business. My daughter's an adult and her choices are hers. Unfortunately, accepting that and being able to butt out are two different things. So I'll just say this. Be very careful. Jade comes across as being tough as nails, but—"

"She's not. Not really." Liam was only just beginning to understand there were aspects of Jade he'd never detected before, injured parts that would take time to heal.

Sawyer paused. "You might not plan to hurt her, but she can be injured just the same."

For a moment, Liam considered opening up to Sawyer. Telling him about the fake fling, Jade moving in, his intentions for the future.

Then he reconsidered. His feelings for Jade were too fresh, too confusing even for Liam. Until he sorted out exactly how he was progressing from here, he'd hold his peace.

"I'll be careful."

Sawyer nodded and, for a moment, Liam thought he'd say more. Mercifully, he didn't. "Guess I'll head over to Compass Ranch."

"Goodbye, Sheriff."

Sawyer walked back to his patrol car without another word. Twice, he hesitated, and Liam braced himself, expecting Jade's father to change his mind, to lose his cool, to come back and punch the shit out of him. He'd seen the marks on his daughter's neck and legs, the light bruises on her wrists. Liam wasn't sure he'd have been able to show as much restraint if the tables had been turned. If it had been his daughter on the couch.

Finally, Sawyer made it to the car. He started it and pulled away.

Liam took a deep breath, then walked back into the house. Jade was still asleep. He grinned at her ability to snooze through anything. Bombs going off wouldn't rouse the woman. He'd have to get two cups of coffee in her before she'd even start to wake up.

He knelt beside the couch and lightly brushed her hair away from her face. Her eyes opened slowly, focusing on him for only a second before taking in the rest of the room.

"Did my dad leave?"

Liam nodded.

"Is he pissed?"

He shrugged. "I don't think so."

A crease formed in Jade's brow as she considered his reply. "He didn't take a swing at you?"

"You expected him to?"

She nodded.

"Thanks for coming to my defense."

Her grin was smug, too pleased as she sarcastically said, "Any time."

Liam stroked her cheek, loving the soft sigh his touch provoked. She was calmer in the morning. Most of the time, Jade stormed through life moving quickly, almost frantically, as if she was always late for something.

He preferred this woman. The one in no hurry to go anywhere. The one who didn't stiffen up at his gentle caresses.

"So Dad really wasn't mad?"

He chuckled at her surprise, even though he'd expected the same response from Sawyer. "Nope. It was all very civil."

"Jade closed her eyes and sighed. "That's boring."

Liam laughed. "You hussy. You really are sorry he didn't punch me, aren't you?"

A mischievous grin appeared as she rolled over onto her back. The sheet pooled around her waist, leaving her breasts bare for his perusal. The sexy woman didn't have a modest bone in her body as she let him look his fill.

"Given the way you've been manhandling me lately, I wouldn't have had a problem if Dad felt the need to defend my honor." While her face was still playful, he suspected there was some seriousness to her words. It would take Jade a damn long time to admit—even to herself—that she enjoyed being dominated sexually. She was too headstrong, willful and independent to accept that truth easily.

"Sorry to disappoint you."

"Oh, that's okay. There's still time. I do have three uncles, four rambunctious male cousins, not to mention Daniel, Wyatt and Clayton in my arsenal. I'm not worried. You'll get yours eventually."

He shook his head, wondering how much danger he was in. While he figured he was safe with Daniel, the uncles, cousins and other ranch hands definitely might take exception to the rough way he'd handled Jade last night should the details ever escape.

"Get up, Jade. I want to finish this conversation in my bed. Or better yet, I'd like to *not* finish it there."

Jade stretched lazily but made no move to rise. "I think I'm going to head on home."

Liam reached out and cupped her breast. He'd been waiting for this. Expecting it. "Aren't you forgetting something? For the next two months, you're living here."

She scowled. "I can't be held accountable for anything I agreed to while under the influence of sex. You coerced me with orgasms. Therefore I'm not staying here."

He squeezed her breast roughly, loving the way her body responded. Jade flushed and he could feel her heart begin to race. She tried to covertly squeeze her legs together under the blanket, but he saw the action just the same. "Be a good girl, Jade, or I'll show you what happens to bad ones."

His taunt had the desired reaction. She knocked his hand away from her breast and sat up, laughing. "God, you're an arrogant prick. You wish you had that much control over me."

She stood, walking across the room in search of her clothing. He waited until she bent over to pick up her jeans before reacting. She pretended to dislike his dominance, but he knew better.

Reaching for her arm, he pulled her upright, then tugged her against his chest. She put up a fight, struggling. Jade was a physical woman—in everything she did—from her chores around the ranch to her ability to break up fights in the bar. It was little wonder she craved that strength and aggression in the bedroom as well.

Liam managed to lift her, hoisting her over his shoulder as Jade pummeled his back. He was reminded of the night of their first kiss at Spurs. In the foyer, he spotted some new straps he'd purchased at a supply store. He grinned as he grabbed them, suddenly finding a more useful purpose for them.

Climbing the stairs, Jade rained a nonstop torrent of nasty names at him, but Liam didn't bother to speak again until they reached his bedroom. He tossed her onto the bed, prepared to counter any attack. She didn't disappoint him when she leapt up immediately.

It took every ounce of strength he had to push her onto her back on the bed. Using his entire body to hold her to the mattress, he called on his rodeo background to help him subdue his wild filly. When Jade realized his intent was to bind her, she kicked the fight into high gear, managing to land two hard blows to the side of his head before he captured her hands. He bound both of them with one of his straps and secured them to the headboard.

He paused. "What's your safe word?"

"Fearless."

"You gonna say it?"

Jade paused. For a moment, he thought she might. Then she shook her head. "No. I'm not."

It was just as he suspected. She liked the fight.

With her hands fastened to the bed, he slid lower, still using his thighs to hold her immobile. Twisting, he tied straps to her ankles. Holding tightly to the bindings, he crawled off the foot of the bed and secured her legs, spread eagle to the bottom posts.

Jade's breathing was loud, her entire body flushed with the exertion. "Had your fun?"

He had to hand it to her. Even defeated, Jade never gave in. Her voice was strong, almost mocking. He might have her tied to his bed, but it would take more than a few straps to hold her.

He crossed his arms, refusing to show weakness, but the intimidating pose only made her laugh. "Ooo, look at you, Mr. Tough Guy."

He smiled, enjoying their game of wills. Jade challenged him, kept him on his toes. Life with her would never be dull, predictable.

Kneeling between her outstretched legs, he countered her strong words with soft touches. Liam lightly stroked her clit, pleased by how well he'd tied her. Jade tried to shake off his fingers, but the straps left her very little wiggle room—literally.

He ran his fingers along her wet pussy, traveling straight to her ass. He circled her anus, using the moisture he'd gathered from her aroused body as he pushed a single finger in to the first knuckle.

Jade gasped and tried to move once more. Liam noticed the tenor of her struggles changed. He didn't think her motions were driven by the desire to escape anymore.

"Move in with me. Just for a little while."

"Why?"

He paused briefly. "What?"

"Why do you want me to stay here? And don't tell me it's just for sex. You know as well as I do, now that we've opened that floodgate, there's precious little—including time and place—that will stop us from coming together."

She was too savvy, too perceptive to buy his lame excuses. He should have known better, but he was thinking with the wrong head these days.

He studied her face, then decided it might be time to start clueing her in to some of his intentions. "You said a real relationship between us could never work. That we fight too much."

Jade wiggled her bound hands, drawing his attention to them as if to say her current position proved that very point.

He ignored her actions. "You're wrong."

She frowned. "So what? Neither of us is looking for anything long-term. Why does it matter?"

"It just does." He was hanging himself out to dry with every word he spoke. Yet part of him wanted her to see what was going on, to understand exactly what was at stake.

Jade fell silent for several moments, uncertain how to reply to Liam's admission. Something had shaken loose in him last night. She'd noticed it in the hospital, as they waited for word of Bruce's condition.

She'd tried to dismiss his overblown reaction to the accident as the result of an adrenaline rush. Something they could erase with hot, rough sex.

Only the remedy had backfired. Rather than calming Liam down, it seemed to ignite even more of this previously unseen possessiveness.

The same response from any other man on earth would have had her kicking the guy to the curb, reading him the riot act for thinking he could actually attempt to stake a claim on her.

But for some reason, that didn't hold true for Liam. She was experiencing an unfamiliar tug. Part of her actually liked that he'd been so afraid of losing her that he freaked out. It warmed some long-cold spaces inside her. His possession didn't feel stifling or threatening or overwhelming. It just felt…good.

Which was bad. Regardless of his opinion, she knew herself—knew them—well enough to know they were skirting a dangerous line. She didn't do relationships. Had never managed to date anyone successfully for more than a few weeks. Something about the concept of forever caused her chest to tighten with fear and she couldn't shake that.

She wouldn't live her life like Vivi, who'd spent more than two decades with a broken heart, longing for the man she'd loved and lost. Her Granddaddy JD had succumbed to cancer before Jade was even born. Her grandmother had spent Jade's entire lifetime with that gaping hole left behind when he died. Jade could only begin to imagine how unbearable that pain and loneliness was for Vivi. Though she'd never spoken it aloud, sometimes Jade wondered if Vivi's memory loss was actually a coping mechanism, a way for her grandmother to forget the man she missed so much.

Jade wouldn't sign on for something like that. Not even for Liam. And she couldn't believe he'd want to either. After all, hadn't he just spent the last eight years of his life mourning for Celia? He couldn't seriously want to take a chance on more pain, more loss. He was just having a weak moment, feeling lonely. The mood would pass soon enough. It had to.

While she loved Liam as a friend, she refused to stand in as a replacement for his true love. She may not long for marriage or commitment, but by the same token, she wouldn't play runner-up to the woman who would always hold Liam's heart.

She studied his face. Forced herself to really see him. His eyes were as familiar to her as her own and she had always been very good at reading the expressions she found there. Right now, she saw hope laced with fear and a fair bit of confusion residing in his dark brown eyes.

He was her best friend and she was going to hurt him. Badly. She knew that as sure as she knew Liam's favorite meal was chipped beef gravy on pancakes.

She also knew nothing was going to change that outcome. They'd started something that neither of them could stop now. She would simply have to hold him to the time limit. Pray that two months would be enough for their strange moods to pass. She'd get over her blues, Liam would recover from his loneliness and they'd move on.

"Fine. I'll go home this afternoon and pack some clothes."

Liam's gaze narrowed. Clearly he was suspicious. She didn't blame him. She wasn't exactly famous for her ability to give in easily. However, in the past, she'd never felt this pure, straight-to-the-bone terror before.

She agreed to his demand because it was the quickest way to make him stop talking.

Liam moved over her, caging her beneath him with his hands on the mattress by her sides. "Are you saying that just so I'll untie you?"

She shook her head. "I don't want you to free me. At least, not yet." She gave him a suggestive wink, hoping to lift the heaviness surrounding them.

Liam didn't take the bait, his expression still distrusting. "Can you take a few weeks off from Compass Ranch?"

"Why would I do that?"

"I want you to work here, with me, with Fearless."

If he'd made the same offer any other day, she would have hooted and hollered and danced the Texas two-step. However, now she questioned the reason behind the offer. Did he think she would try to weasel out of living with him? Was he trying to sweeten the pot?

While the extra incentive wasn't necessary, she grabbed it anyway. "I'm sure I can. School's out for the summer and there are a bunch of high school kids looking for work. I'll talk my uncles into hiring a couple while I come here. If you're sure that's what you really want."

The seriousness on his face dissolved, replaced by the first genuine smile she'd seen since he'd carried her to the bedroom. "I've wanted to lure you away from Compass Ranch for years, but I figured you'd never leave the family business."

"What girl can resist a raging, powerful bull?"

Liam laughed. "I realize you're not talking about me, but I'm just arrogant enough to pretend otherwise."

With that issue resolved, Liam gave up his gentle touches, opting instead for something that couldn't be described as anything less than forceful. Wonderful. One night in and Jade was already addicted to Liam's dominance.

At some point, she'd have to sit and analyze what the hell it was about this type of sex that made her toes curl with excitement and her pussy clench with need. But for right now, she didn't give a shit about the psychology.

Liam pressed three fingers deep, causing her head to spin and her heart to race. She tried to move toward his intense drives, but he knew his way around straps. He'd secured her to the bed tightly. The idea of being helpless beneath him left her breathless, hungry in ways she'd never experienced before. He toyed with her clit, stroking her slow, then fast. Gentle, then hard.

"God. So good." She closed her eyes, ready to give in to her climax when Liam withdrew.

When she looked at him, she found him kneeling between her outstretched thighs, his face suddenly strict, stern. More moisture found its way to her sex.

"Not yet."

She scoffed. "I'll come whenever I want, cowboy."

Liam shook his head, cueing her in to the stupidity of her assertion. Without his help, she was screwed. And not in a good way.

"You want to reconsider that comment?"

She blew out an exasperated breath. He'd tied her to his bed and pushed every hot button inside her. Now he had her over a barrel and they both knew it. "Maybe," she conceded begrudgingly. Reconciling the two extremes in her personality would never come easily.

"There's nothing wrong with giving up control every now and then, Jade. I know what you need, what you want. Why's it so hard for you to let me give it to you?"

"I have no idea. It just is."

Rather than respond, Liam left the bed, crossing to his closet. He dug around for a few minutes before returning with a necktie.

"Planning to go to church to pray for some answers?" she taunted.

He chuckled. "Nope. Gonna help you curb that loose tongue of yours." Liam knelt on the bed by her side, putting a knot in the tie, then using it as a gag.

Jade tried to resist it, but her struggles were pointless. Once it was in place, he shucked off his jeans and returned to his spot between her legs.

He pointed to her right hand. "Raise two fingers. Give me the peace sign."

She frowned, confused, but did as he asked.

Liam looked pleased. "Since you can't say the safe word, that's the signal. Do that and I'll stop."

Jade pulled the fingers down quickly, drawing her hand into a fist.

"Maybe that gag will stop you from trying to give orders. Now. I'm going to fuck you, Jade. First with my fingers and then with my dick. You're not going to come until I tell you to. If you do, I'll untie your legs, flip you over and use my belt on you."

Her pussy clenched, her face giving away exactly how much his threats weren't scaring her.

"Jesus, Jade. You're killing me."

While she enjoyed the way he exerted his power over her, she loved being able to do the same. She may have the quieter role, but the truth was she held just as many cards as Liam, if not more.

She closed her eyes and moaned when Liam curled his fingers inside her, stroking her g-spot. Stars formed behind her lowered lids and once again, the desire to come overwhelmed her. Jade began to give in to it, but Liam was too in tune with her body's signals.

He withdrew.

She shot him a dirty look that was met with one raised eyebrow and a taunting expression that basically said *I dare you.*

Jade took a deep breath through her nose, trying to still the demon inside her clawing for freedom.

Liam smiled when he recognized she was in control of her needs, then returned to torment her some more. When her orgasm approached yet again, Jade fought with everything she had to keep it at bay.

Liam didn't make it easy on her. He continued to thrust his fingers deeply, making sure to hit just the right spot every single time. Jade swallowed heavily, her mouth dry. Her body started to tremble, yet she remained strong.

Finally, after a century and a half, Liam granted her reprieve. "Come."

She exploded. Splintered. Shattered.

It was painful. Beautiful.

She wanted to scream his name, felt the need to wrap her arms around him so he could hold her to the planet. As it was, she'd been catapulted into space, rocketed into orbit. It reminded her of her first time on a roller coaster. The incredible trip up and down the track had been terrifying. Exhilarating. The second she stepped out of the car, her feet touching earth, she'd known she would want to ride again. And again.

It was the same now.

Liam tugged the gag out of her mouth. She started to speak, but he was there, kissing her, his tongue plunging against hers.

"Come inside me," she whispered, surprised by the husky, sexy tone of her own voice. It sounded foreign to her.

Liam released her legs, bending her knees to open

her completely. "Wrap your ankles around my waist and hang on."

Captured by the straps at her wrists and Liam's powerful thrusts, Jade gave in to the moment as another orgasm claimed her. Then another. Soon, Liam was with her, hot, thick jets of come scalding her, filling her.

Right now, right here, she was his.

And it was perfect.

Chapter Seven

Jade peeked around the hospital door. "Knock knock. You still alive?"

Bruce gestured for her to enter. "'Bout time you got your ass over here to visit me. I'm bored out of my mind and the food tastes like shit. I'm gonna need you to make a run for a cheeseburger and fries."

Jade rolled her eyes and claimed the seat beside Bruce's bed, her guilt over not making it to visit him yesterday fading quickly in the face of his demands. She'd intended to come see her boss first thing yesterday, but her day had unraveled in ways she'd never have been able to predict. It began with the early visit from her father, followed by the few hours she spent tied to Liam's bed and ending with Liam escorting her to her cabin to help her pack, then the two of them eating a late dinner nude in his kitchen before moving the party back to the bedroom.

"No. I've been telling you for weeks to go to the doctor and you ignored me. Healthy meals are your punishment."

"Dammit, Jade, I'm a dying man. The least you could do is give me my last request."

She snorted. "You lying jackass. I saw your doctor and you're fine. You've just got a hole in your stomach, for pity's sake."

"And high blood pressure," Bruce added, as if that would convince her to do his bidding. "Probably caused by you and your sassy mouth at work."

"It's caused by eating trash and smoking."

Bruce scowled, his grumpy expression too familiar to her. "The least you could have done was smuggle me in some goddamn beef jerky."

Jade reached into the pocket of her shorts and pulled out a Ziploc with two strips of his favorite treat. "Here."

"Two lousy pieces? You couldn't bring the whole pack?"

Jade yanked the baggie out of his hand. "Ungrateful asshole." She opened it, pulled a slice out and proceeded to eat it. "Just for that, you only get one."

"Aw hell, stop fooling around. Give me that."

She handed him the jerky. She shouldn't give him the stuff at all, but she knew Bruce well enough to comprehend that two days in the hospital without a Whopper, a beer or a cigarette probably had him contemplating a jump from his second-story hospital window. Jerky seemed like the lesser evil of all her boss's vices.

He chewed, closing his eyes as if she'd just delivered pure heaven.

"You feeling okay?"

Bruce shrugged. "They're going to have to put a stent in my heart. Apparently it's an easy procedure. In and out surgery. Piece of cake."

Jade hated the idea of her unhealthy boss having to go under the knife at all. "I guess that's good. What about the blood pressure?"

"They're trying to bring it down with medicine and diet." It was clear Bruce wasn't fond of their methods. She worried about what would happen when he left the hospital. He lived alone, with no wife to keep an eye on him and force him to behave. Jade made a mental note to stop by his house after he was released to bring him some fruit and vegetables. Maybe she could recruit Hope to help her fix him some healthy meals he could heat up easily. Jade sucked in the kitchen, but her cousin was an amazing cook.

"You saved my life, Jade."

She waved her boss's words away. "Not really. Liam did most of the heavy lifting."

Bruce grinned and patted his oversized paunch. "Guess I could stand to lose a few."

Jade raised an eyebrow. "Gee. Ya think so?"

"You know, Jade, I never got married or had kids. I was never interested in any of that shit. But I'd like to think if I'd ever had a daughter, she'd be the complete opposite of you."

Jade snorted with mirth, laughing so loudly the noise pulled a nurse in to check on them. Once they'd assured the woman no one was screaming in pain, the nurse left as she and Bruce dissolved into laughter again.

"God, you're a bastard, Bruce. But I do love you and your fat ass."

Bruce reached out and patted her hand. It was the only time her boss had ever shown her any sort of affection. "I love you too, Jade."

She waited for him to add some irreverent joke to take away the seriousness of the moment, but instead he fell silent and smiled at her.

His sincerity took her unaware as tears formed in her eyes. She cleared her throat and stood up quickly, under the guise of tidying up a few magazines that were scattered around the room.

"Hello?"

Jade turned around, surprised to find Hope and Vivi standing at the door. "What are you two doing here?"

Hope smiled. "Vivi had a check-up this morning. She insisted we stop in to see how you're doing, Bruce. Hope you don't mind."

Jade grinned at the change in her gruff boss's demeanor with Vivi's arrival. When it had just been Jade in the room, he'd remained slouched and sloppy-looking, not bothering to sit up. The second Vivi had entered the room, Bruce had pushed himself to an upright position, finger-combed his hair and straightened his sheets.

"Awful nice of you to stop in, Vicky."

Vivi claimed the chair beside Bruce. Jade could see by the happy expression in her grandmother's eyes that today was a good day. Hope plopped down on the small couch beneath the window while Jade continued to hover near the bed.

"I was worried when I heard about the car accident. Has my granddaughter been looking after you?"

Bruce nodded. "She's doing her best, but I've been told by more than a few of the hospital staff that I'm not exactly a model patient."

Vivi laughed. "Good for you. Life is no fun when you behave."

"Vivi," Jade admonished. "Don't encourage him."

"JD was a terrible patient as well. It's not easy for strong, independent men to feel beholden to anyone else. So I'll tell you what I always told him, Bruce. Suck it up."

Bruce smiled. "Yes, ma'am. If JD could do it, I'll try my best."

Jade nearly got whiplash, checking to make sure

it was still her boss lying in the hospital bed. She'd never heard such quiet politeness out of him. Bruce noticed her surprise and shot her a dirty look.

Bruce had never spoken to her about JD, but it was clear from his conversation with Vivi that he thought highly of her grandfather.

Jade listened as Bruce and Vivi briefly reminisced about the good old days. Apparently JD and Bruce's father had been best friends growing up.

"I didn't realize you knew my granddaddy," Jade said.

Vivi patted Bruce's hand kindly. "Bruce is a few years older than Silas. When he was just a little thing, he was fascinated by anything and everything to do with cows. His parents were in the process of opening Spurs. Back then, it was more diner than bar. JD suggested Bruce spend the summer with us while they got things up and running."

"To keep me from being underfoot while my parents worked," Bruce added.

Vicky grinned. "You followed JD day after day on that ranch, helping out. I always wondered if you missed your calling by being a barman. You made a fair hand."

Bruce chuckled. "I was six years old, Vicky. I'm pretty sure I was more annoyance than assistance."

"JD loved having you there. In fact, I got pregnant with Silas that fall. JD said having you around made him realize how much he wanted some sons of his own."

Bruce grew quiet, a sadness coming into his eyes. "JD was an amazing man, Vicky. Not too many days go by where I don't think about him."

Vivi nodded. "I miss him too."

Jade recognized the loneliness on Vivi's face far too well.

Vivi and Bruce continued telling stories, sharing memories of people long since gone. Jade glanced over when she felt Hope tug on her shirt and tilt her head toward the door. Jade followed her cousin to the small alcove as Bruce chuckled over some gossip Vivi shared.

"Thanks for stopping by with Vivi, Hope. She appears to be just what the doctor ordered. Bruce looks downright giddy. Unless, of course, that's indigestion."

Hope grinned. "He's a gruff old guy, isn't he? I'm not sure I'd like to call him my boss."

Hope had always been the sweet one of the cousins, kind and quiet. One tongue-lashing from Bruce probably would have devastated Hope, who never wanted to disappoint anyone. Lucky for Jade, she was immune to Bruce's rough ways.

"Don't be fooled. Under that miserable exterior, he's pure marshmallow. You just have to dig really, really deep."

"What's going on with you and Liam?"

Jade blinked, surprised by Hope's abrupt change of subject. "What?"

"Sterling said you packed a bag yesterday afternoon, that you're moving in with him. And Daddy says you've asked for some time off to start working at Circle H."

Jade blew out a long breath. It never took long for news to spread in her family. She'd only talked to Colby and Silas about taking a few weeks off this morning. "I'm going to start doing some work for Liam. Help him train Fearless and a few of the bucking broncs. You know how much I love that."

Hope crossed her arms. "You don't have to live with the man to do that. It's not like his ranch and ours are so far apart."

Jade had been in such a tailspin over Liam's

desire for a summer fling and then his insistence that she stay with him, she'd failed to figure out how she would explain things to her cousins or her parents. Or her aunts and uncles.

She'd asked Colby and Silas about the mini-vacation, not daring to mention the brief change of address as well. And she'd managed to avoid Sterling, who had been busting at the seams to question her. Fortunately, Liam hadn't believed she'd follow through on her promise to move in, so he'd shadowed her as she packed, no doubt expecting her to run. As a result, he'd protected her from Sterling's inquisition and bought her a bit of time. Time she'd squandered with sex rather than thinking about the answers to questions that were bound to come.

Maybe she was lucky it was Hope who'd cornered her first. She was, by far, the easiest to flounder for answers with.

"Liam and I are sort of indulging in a friends-with-benefits thing right now."

Hope's eyes widened. "You and Liam? Seriously? Since when?"

Jade tried to decide exactly when it had started. They'd only had sex the night before last, but the whole tenor of their relationship had changed with that kiss at Spurs. "Not quite three weeks ago."

Pure excitement blossomed on Hope's face. Damn. This was bad.

"That's so amazing. I'm so happy for you. The two of you are per—"

"No." Jade raised her hand to cut off the rest of her cousin's words. "We're not perfect or amazing or anything. We're just fucking for a couple of months."

Hope frowned. "You put a time limit on it?"

Jade nodded.

"You can't do that."

Now it was Jade's turn to frown. "Why not?"

"Because it doesn't work like that."

Jade felt the desire to defend her decision, even though she completely agreed with Hope. "Who says?"

Hope reached out to touch her arm. "Jade. Are you sure you're doing the right thing here? I mean, you and Liam have been friends for a really long time. Doesn't this seem sort of impulsive? Reckless?"

That's exactly what it was. It was what Liam had offered right from the beginning. And while Jade had longed to shake things up in her life, she hadn't meant to go quite so far.

"We're going to be fine, Hope. The two of us have set very clear boundaries." At least she hoped they had.

Hope didn't seem convinced, but mercifully, she let it drop. "So how are you going to explain this to everyone?"

Jade shrugged. "What I just told you doesn't work?"

Hope laughed. "Not if you don't want your dad to kill Liam."

Jade didn't bother to tell Hope her father already knew she'd spent the night with Liam. He'd managed to escape unscathed, so maybe it wouldn't be so bad. "What would you suggest?"

"Just tell everyone you're dating. That's what they're going to assume anyway given your new sleepover status."

For some reason, that lie—though simpler than the truth—rubbed against the grain. "Can't I just say we're shacking up for sex? Why do I have to pretend there's a relationship involved?"

Hope bit her lower lip, a sure sign her cousin was worried. "What would be so terrible about going out with Liam for real? The two of you have a long history and my mom always says the best relationships are born from friendship."

Jade fell back on the same excuses she'd offered Liam. "We fight all the time, Hope. While he's never said as much, I think my foul mouth and loud laughter sort of grate on his nerves. I'm way too fond of my independence and not about to give that up for anyone. Besides, I'm not his type. He goes for petite, giggly and girly. I'm none of those and don't intend to ever be. I mean...you have to admit, I'm nothing like Celia Woods."

Hope squeezed her arm. "I think you'd make some man a wonderful wife."

Jade feigned a shudder. "You didn't really just use the W word on me, did you?"

"I wish you'd stop swearing you'll never get married. What's so wrong with falling in love and spending the rest of your life with someone?" Hope's softly spoken question left Jade floundering for an answer. In the past, her determination to remain single had never wavered because she'd never been tempted. Liam was definitely messing with her head. Making her reflect on things she didn't want to consider.

Jade didn't feel comfortable telling Hope why she preferred the idea of living alone. Given Hope's belief in true love and forever, Jade suspected it would trouble her cousin to know how deep Jade's fear of loss ran. The fact remained it was something that had always been there inside her and she didn't see it ever going away.

While she could handle closeness when it came to her family and her friends, the second a guy got too close, she felt herself closing up, suffocating on panic.

If she were the type of person who could deal with personal introspection, maybe she'd find an answer, but she didn't have the time or energy to delve too deeply into shit like that. It was easier to just accept this was who she was, chalk it up as a personality flaw and move on.

She was saved when Vivi approached them. "You ready to go, Lucy?"

Hope's face fell as their grandmother called her by the wrong name. Though it happened more and more frequently these days, it never got any easier for them to admit that while Vivi was still with them physically, her mind was failing fast.

"Sure." Hope didn't correct Vivi. It upset their grandmother too much when she realized she'd slipped up. It put her on edge and caused her to stop talking for a few hours just so she wouldn't make any more mistakes. They'd all decided to roll with the mistaken identities in hopes of saving Vivi from suffering any extra anxiety. "Goodbye, Bruce. Hope you feel better soon," Hope called out from the doorway.

Jade waved as they left, understanding Hope's hasty departure. When Vivi's mind began to drift, they appreciated the importance of getting her home and out of public settings.

Jade had just returned to Bruce's bedside when she heard a male voice at the doorway.

"Hey Bruce. How you feeling?"

Jade turned, surprised to find Liam there. She gave him a flirty wink. "What are you doing? Following me around? Do I need to put a restraining order on you to stop this stalking?"

Liam chuckled as he walked up and patted her ass. "You wish. Bucky nearly cut his damn thumb off with the band saw this morning."

"Oh my God. Is he okay?"

Liam shrugged. "Actually I'm exaggerating to make the story more interesting. It's only a little cut. I drove him here. His sister just got to his room. She'll take him home after they finish putting five or six stitches in."

"Well. That's good, I guess."

"Did you want to apologize for accusing me of being a stalker?"

He looked so damn cocky and amused, she was tempted to dig her hands into the back pockets of his sexy jeans and do a little stalking of her own. She could bounce quarters on his tight, gorgeous ass. Instead, she said, "Bite me."

"With pleasure," he murmured.

"Jesus," Bruce muttered. "Finally gave in to it, I see."

Jade scowled, annoyed that she'd forgotten to shield herself in front of her boss. She and Liam really were going to have to work out what to tell people about them. "What are you talking about?"

"You two have been sniffing around each other for years. 'Bout time you stopped denying it."

Despite Hope's advice, Jade never took the easy route. "We're just screwing around, Bruce. It's nothing serious. Pretty sure it'll die out before the summer ends."

She expected Liam to back her up, but she was greeted by silence. She glanced at him, discovering her answer had obviously pissed him off. The story would only work if they were on the same page, and it didn't appear they were.

Rather than start an argument, Liam turned to Bruce. "When do you think they'll spring you from this joint?"

Bruce shrugged. "Not soon enough. Doc said two days at the earliest if I behave myself. Not sure what the fuck he thinks I'm going to do. They've got goddamn Attila the Hun out there pretending to be a nurse. Woman watches me like a hawk."

Jade rolled her eyes, but Liam laughed.

"Hey, do me favor, Liam. Jade's going to be running the bar the next couple of nights. You mind hanging out after closing to make sure she gets to her car okay?"

Jade exploded. "Are you kidding me, Bruce? I don't need a babysitter. And I certainly don't need Liam hovering all night."

Liam ignored her outburst. "Sure thing, Bruce. No problem."

Jade turned toward Liam. "Listen, cowboy. I don't want—"

"Okay. Everybody out."

Jade turned to see Nurse Attila walking in. "Mr. Coulten is scheduled for some tests and I need to get him upstairs."

"See you later, Bruce. And don't worry about the bar. Jade and I will take care of everything." Liam added just enough emphasis to the *I* part to let her know he was trying to tweak her even more.

Jade shot Liam a dirty look before adding her goodbyes. "I'll visit again tomorrow. Okay, Bruce?"

"Sure. And Jade. Don't be stingy when you come back." He gave her a meaningful look that told her she'd better come armed with more jerky or there would be hell to pay.

Because she was pissed off at him for saddling her with a caretaker, she decided to get back a bit of her own. "I'm not making any promises. I might not be able to escape my babysitter long enough to shop. See you tomorrow."

She left the room with a grin as Liam followed her out. They hadn't made it two steps into the hallway before she felt his large hand engulf her upper arm, pulling her to a stop.

"What's your hurry?" Liam asked.

"I have errands to run."

"They can wait." Liam propelled her farther down the hall, opening the door to a storage closet before pushing her in. He followed, then closed the door.

"Oh wow. This is classy."

Liam gripped her hips and pulled her toward him. Even through their clothing, she could feel his hard-on. "Never promised you class."

His hands delved under her shirt, cupping her breasts firmly.

"You realize I only left your bed a few hours ago."

He lifted her shirt, looking down at the skin he'd exposed. "That long? Damn."

He bent his head and sucked on her nipples through her bra. The lace and pressure of his mouth rasped against the suddenly sensitive nubs.

Jade tugged at Liam's dark hair, holding him in place as he deepened the suction. "Harder."

Her softly whispered word seemed to offer Liam the permission he needed. He straightened and turned her away from him. Reaching around her waist, he worked free the button and lowered the zipper on her shorts. Liam pushed them and her panties to the ground, then pressed on her upper back, bending her over.

"Grab that shelf in front of you. And try to be quiet."

She didn't take him to task for his highhandedness. The few hours they'd spent apart seemed like an eternity to her as well.

Liam quickly unfastened his jeans and freed his cock. She glanced over her shoulder, watching as he placed his dick at the opening of her sex.

He grinned when he found her wet. "Somebody's ready."

She shrugged. "Don't flatter yourself. There are a lot of hot doctors around here."

He chuckled, and conversation ceased as Liam slowly thrust inside her. Jade closed her eyes, trying not to admit to herself how much she craved this. Him. They'd only spent two nights together, but it was enough to prove he was the best lover she'd ever had. Enough to make her want more.

Liam's grip on her hips tightened when he was fully seated. He paused. "Ready?"

She nodded, hoping she'd be able to remain silent. Too many times last night, she'd yelled out with her release. She'd never been particularly vocal in bed before, but it was nearly impossible to stay quiet with Liam.

He withdrew for only a second before plunging back in. Jade tightened her hold on the shelf as Liam drove into her hard. He used his hands to drag her toward him on every forward thrust, increasing the intensity.

Jade cried out, louder than she intended. If anyone had been passing the closet at that moment, there would have been no denying what was going on inside. One of Liam's hands left her hip. He used it to grip her hair, pulling her upright.

"What did I say about not making any noise?" he whispered in her ear.

Though his pounding was less powerful in this new position, his cock stroked her g-spot and she released another moan, unable to hold in the sound.

Liam covered her mouth with his hand, making her feel captured, claimed. It drove her arousal even higher. She arched her back as Liam continued to thrust.

He reached around her waist, the fingers of his free hand finding her clit. Jade jerked at the initial, too-soft touch.

"You're going to come, Jade. And you're not going to make a single sound while you do it. Understand?"

He was destined to be disappointed. There was no way she could remain silent. Even now, as his fingers stroked her clit, she couldn't hold back the little mewls of desire.

"You'll be completely quiet, Jade. I mean it."

She shook her head, dislodging his hand briefly. "And if I'm not?"

"I'll drive you back to my house and tie you to my bed. I'll put a vibrator in your pussy set on low, a plug in your ass, and I'll leave you there, on the verge of an orgasm with no means of relief for the rest of the day. Any questions?"

Why did that threat sound so hot to her?

Liam didn't wait for her reply. Instead, he pressed her forward once more, increasing the pace of his fucking until he found that incredible edge—that place where pleasure and pain blended, the combination better than peanut butter and chocolate.

"Liam," she whispered.

"Not a sound," he warned.

She closed her eyes, struggling to hold back her gasping breaths. She was so close, seconds away from exploding. It would be so easy to let go, to set loose the screaming orgasm, but something resisted, longed to please Liam. To show him she could give him what he wanted.

He pressed her clit more firmly and she was lost. Her body trembled forcefully, imploding rather than blasting apart.

It was incredible and he was right there with her. His cock pulsed inside her, filling her with his come and his hold tightened as he murmured her name over and over.

When Jade settled down and began to take notice of her surroundings once more, she was wrapped up in Liam's strong embrace. No doubt she would have dissolved into a puddle of goo on the floor if not for his arms holding her, supporting her.

It took several minutes for her to realize he was speaking, praising her. "God, Jade. So good, baby. You're so amazing."

She longed to stay in his arms, wanted to remain snug, sheltered, safe. It was an alien feeling. Usually at this point in the aftermath of sex, Jade would already be dressed and halfway out the door. With Liam, she wasn't searching for an escape, but rather an excuse to stay.

She forced herself to move back. Liam's face darkened briefly, obviously not happy with her hasty departure.

"Jade." He tried to draw her toward him again, but she dodged his hands, bending down to pull her shorts back on.

She tidied herself without looking at him. "Thanks. I have to admit screwing around in a hospital storage closet is a new one for me. I'll have to add that to my list of crazy sex places."

Liam nodded slowly as he refastened his jeans. "You heading straight to the bar from here?"

"Yeah. I have a few things to do before I open."

Liam brushed her hair away from her face, the touch too familiar, too caring for her peace of mind, so she tried to step around him, anxious to put some space between them and this unfamiliar feeling.

"I'll stop by later tonight and hang around until closing."

"You really don't have to do that."

He grinned, though the look appeared more

grimace than happiness. "Actually, I do."

The expression soothed her ragged nerves. Maybe Liam was experiencing the same sense of unease.

"Suit yourself. I'll see you tonight."

He moved to the right to allow her to pass, but before she could reach the doorknob, he grasped her face and pressed his lips to hers. It was a relatively quick kiss, but Liam made up for it with skill. Pressure and heat combined to tell her there was more behind the buss than just saying goodbye.

Jade's heart had only begun to return to its normal pace, but Liam's kiss set it racing again. When he released her, she struggled to find her bearings.

Liam stroked her cheek gently. "See you later, kiddo."

She swallowed heavily, marveling over how much she didn't want to leave. How the idea of walking away was almost physically painful. What did that mean? "Bye."

The rest of the day she found herself touching her lips, recalling his kiss. By the time they closed up for the night, she was a pent-up ball of desires and need, begging Liam for relief.

They made it as far as his truck in the parking lot before Liam pushed her against the passenger door, taking her in a haze of quick, hard thrusts, clinging hands, breathless demands.

Then they went back to his house, repeating it all in the shower. And again in his bed.

Before dawn appeared on the horizon the next day, Jade knew she was in deep. Liam rolled over, pulling her to him spoon-fashion, his cock slowly sliding in.

Oh, what the hell?

Trouble was her middle name.

Chapter Eight

Jade let the roar of her motorcycle soothe her as she flew along the road between Compass Ranch and Liam's home. A quick glance at the speedometer proved she was pushing ninety. She blew out a frustrated breath, her promise to curb her wilder instincts coming back to her as she quickly slowed down.

For two weeks, Liam had followed through on his vow to spice up her life in style. The lingering sadness she'd felt consumed by at the beginning of the summer had definitely started to wane.

Hell, who was she kidding? It was all but gone. She'd been too busy fucking to remember what was bothering her in the first place. For sixteen nights, Liam had given her orgasm after mind-blowing orgasm, pushing her limits until she wasn't sure she even had any more.

Last night, he'd introduced her to nipple clamps, driving her to a climax simply by playing with her breasts—issuing a sweet blend of soft kisses alternated with tight, stinging pinches. He showered her with so many sensations that her vision blurred and her body trembled. Liam had a way of taking over so completely Jade lost all sense of time and place. She disappeared into a world of Liam's making. One so beautiful and warm and safe, she never wanted to come back to reality.

She'd fought him initially when he'd suggested that they move in together, but now she had to admit that idea had been a stroke of genius. Both of them were fairly hard workers, rising early each morning to do the chores associated with living on a ranch. They'd fallen into a routine, as they'd train the cattle until lunchtime, after which they'd break for food and a quickie. Jade grinned as she recalled all the creative ways Liam had taken her during their midday sexual escapades. They'd initiated nearly every inch of the kitchen and more than their fair share of flat surfaces in various other rooms in the house as well.

After lunch, Jade ran errands or visited her cousins and Vivi before heading into town when it was her night to open Spurs. While Bruce had returned to work, he still wasn't one hundred percent, so more than a few times he'd taken off once Liam showed up. The two of them would close the bar together when she worked late and head home, falling into each other's arms, fucking and sleeping until the sun appeared and they started all over. She should be completely exhausted. Instead, she'd never felt more energetic, exhilarated. Alive.

If she weren't staying at Circle H, Jade wouldn't have had much time to spend with Liam. And *not* seeing him was something she didn't want to consider. She craved his touches, his kisses, his presence. While she hadn't lost sight of the deadline, well aware of the day when all of this would end, she refused to deny herself one minute of the bliss found in Liam's bed until then. There was something about him that was different, though she struggled to put her finger on exactly what.

Today was likely to test the limits they'd drawn. She pulled up in front of the barn and threw down the kickstand on her bike. Her chest was tight and her hands shaking as she walked into the cool shade of the structure, looking for Liam.

"Jade?"

His deep voice came from one of the stalls. She turned to look for him in the shadows. Finally she found him, tossing fresh hay into the corner of a pen. He was shirtless, wearing nothing but his favorite pair of jeans and a cowboy hat. Sprigs of straw clung to the light sheen of sweat on his chest. He looked deliciously male. Just what the doctor ordered.

She glanced around the barn. "Where's Bucky?"

"Out in the north pasture. I thought you were going to visit Vicky."

His question sent a shard of pain through her heart. "I don't want to talk about Vivi."

Her grandmother hadn't recognized her today. Jade was becoming accustomed to that. What had hurt today was her grandmother's fury. She'd lashed out at Jade. Told her she was trespassing. That she had no right to be there. Jade hadn't known what to do, so she'd called Aunt Lucy. Lucy brought some medication, but Vivi has been so agitated by her presence that Jade had decided it would be better to simply leave her grandmother in her aunt's care.

She'd considered riding around until the agony subsided. In the past, flying down the highway too fast, using distance and the roaring of the motorcycle's engine, helped erase the fear, the aching. Today, she'd opted for another cure. Liam.

"Jade," Liam started.

"Is anyone else around?" Her words came out louder, angrier than she intended.

Liam shook his head.

"Good." Jade reached for the hem of her T-shirt, tugging the cotton over her head.

She'd hoped the action would incite a bit of hunger in Liam, but instead he studied her with those cool, calm, too-observant brown eyes. The look pissed her off.

She reached for the hooks on her bra, unfastening them and shrugging off the lace. Still Liam didn't move. She longed for a reaction. Needed it.

"I was speeding on the way here. On my motorcycle. Got her up to ninety."

Finally, his gaze narrowed and she detected the slightest tightening around his jawline. "Is that so?"

She nodded as she worked free the button on her jeans. "Yeah. Then I slowed down and drove carefully the rest of the way here."

Liam frowned, clearly confused by her admission.

"So now I want my prize for good behavior."

"What happened at Compass Ranch, Jade?"

Her temper spiked. "Nothing." She tugged down her pants, kicked off her shoes. Liam was quiet as he perused her naked body. Shyness had never been a part of her personality, so she stood comfortably as he looked.

When he made no move to approach her, she put her hands on her hips. "My reward?"

Liam's gaze returned to her face when she spoke. She was breathing rapidly, standing on a narrow ledge, trying desperately not to fall. She was upset, furious, scared. She hated every single one of those emotions. Needed Liam to wipe them away. To drag her back into the safety of his world. A world where Alzheimer's didn't exist.

"How bad was she?"

She exploded, flying forward. "Fuck you, Liam

Harrison! You promised me! Told me I could come to you!" As she spoke, she shoved him. She needed physical contact and she didn't care if it came through sex or aggression. Both would be ideal.

Liam was a mountain of a man. Her rough push did little more than move the hay clinging to his chest. So she shoved him once more.

Liam captured her arms, tugging her hands behind her back. He squeezed them tightly until she winced, gasped.

"You want a fight, Jade?"

She nodded. Oh God. Hell yeah, she did. She wanted to beat on something, someone, until they felt as shitty as she did.

Liam released her hands. The sudden freedom caught her off-guard. Then he lifted his arms in surrender. "Do your worst."

"Be serious."

"I am."

His invitation irritated her. "I don't hit like a girl, you know. If I punch you, you're going to feel it."

The corners of his lips tipped up, taunting her. "I expect I will. Do it anyway."

She reared back without a second thought and swung, though she pulled back at the last minute, afraid of hurting him.

Liam put his hands on his hips. "Try it again, Jade."

"Liam—"

"One more time. As hard as you can. Then it's my turn."

She swiped her brow with her forearm, wiping away the sweat trickling from her hairline, stinging her eyes. The weatherman predicted today would be the hottest day of the summer. He hadn't lied.

Jade tried to take a steadying breath, but failed.

Her heart was racing, her head pounding. She couldn't take much more of this fucking day. This fucking life.

"Fine." Balling her hand in a fist, she let loose with every ounce of frustration and misery she could muster. Liam reared back when she caught him in the stomach. His loud *oomph* told her she'd hurt him.

Regret appeared. Words of apology forming on her lips. Neither made landfall when Liam gripped her upper arm and dragged her to the corner of the barn. This spot was more open than the stall they'd just left.

Liam picked up some thin cord from a pile of ropes stashed there and looped it around Jade's wrists. His movements were quick, efficient.

He raised her arms, and it was then Jade noticed the hook above her head. Liam attached the rope to it, the height forcing her to stand on tiptoe. Her head swam at how effectively he'd managed to capture her, render her helpless.

Strangely, the fear she'd felt when she left Compass Ranch started to wane. One of these days she'd have to figure out why Liam's bondage made her feel safe rather than terrified. Clearly something was broken inside of her. Little surprise there. She'd felt out of step with the world for most of her life.

Liam stood a few feet away, studying his work in silence.

She didn't feel the need to break it, to fill it with mindless chatter. She reveled in these quiet moments with Liam when the only thing she had to consider in the world was what he would do next.

He stepped closer, the heat from his skin combining with hers. Though it was cooler in the shade of the barn, Jade suspected the temperature was still pushing ninety, probably more.

"Feel better?" he asked.

She shook her head.

Though his brow was creased, concern written on his face, Liam never denied her, never balked at her desires or criticized her for them. He reached up and cupped her bare breast, squeezing the flesh that was still tender from their lovemaking the previous night.

The reminder of the tight clamps sent a surge of arousal to her pussy. She wished he had them with him now. She tried to admonish him when he released her breast, but Liam shushed her.

"No, Jade. No complaints. No demands. You're going to take what I offer or I'll cut you down from there and end things right now."

She shook her head rapidly. "Don't stop." Her mind silently added *ever*, though she didn't dare speak the word aloud.

"Then trust me to know what you need."

She did. Completely. That thought soothed her.

"Good," Liam murmured just before he placed a soft kiss on her lips. While she generally loved his kisses, she didn't need his comfort today. She longed for something more powerful, more brutal.

Liam must have understood because he kept the contact brief. Then he stepped behind her. Jade didn't bother to turn her head to watch.

Trust.

His hand struck her ass hard, the strong blow sending sparks of pain mixed with need throughout her body. He didn't pause, didn't give her time to recover as his hand struck her flesh again. She had no awareness of the passage of time. It was irrelevant. She wanted to stay here forever.

The spanking stopped too soon as Liam's rough hands burrowed between her legs from behind. He pushed two fingers inside her sex, pumping rapidly. Jade's head fell forward, the first of her orgasms imminent. Weeks with Liam had made her greedy, taught her to expect multiple orgasms rather than being appeased with one lukewarm climax in a night.

Liam continued to finger-fuck her, using his free hand to stroke her clit. The combination worked as she cried out his name. Liam let her ride out the storm before thrusting her straight back into it. He pinched her clit, using his now-drenched fingers to fuck her ass. He'd bought her a butt plug during her first weekend at his place, introducing her to the magic of anal sex.

The forbidden act, the pinch, the pain and the pleasure blended together to make it one of her favorite things.

"Fuck me. There." He'd told her to make no demands, but she sucked at following orders.

"No."

She groaned when he pressed deeper into her ass. "Please."

"No lube. It would hurt like hell."

"I don't care."

He cut off her pleas with several hard thrusts. "I do."

Jade lifted one leg, twisting her foot to relieve the cramps forming there. Her toes weren't used to supporting her for so long.

Liam must have noticed her distress as the hook holding her arms up lowered slightly, allowing her to stand with her feet flat on the ground.

"Better?"

She nodded.

"Good. You're going to need steady footing."

She twisted to look at him as he moved away from her. Her breath caught when he took a riding crop down from a rack hanging on the wall.

He didn't approach her, merely watched her, his arms hanging by his sides. "You asked me to use this on you a few nights ago."

Summer Fling

She licked her lips, fear and arousal pulsing through her so powerfully she felt certain she'd fall to her knees without his ropes holding her up. "I did. You said later."

He looked down at the crop in his hand, and for the first time since they'd embarked on their affair, Jade sensed hesitance on his part.

"Liam, you don't have to if..."

He glanced at her. "If what? If I don't want to? I do. That doesn't scare you?"

She shook her head. "Nothing you've done has frightened me."

Liam closed his eyes momentarily, then he captured her gaze again as he walked closer. "One of these days we're going to discuss this."

She knew what he was talking about. It was clear they shared similar kinks, but rather than talk about it, they'd jumped in with both feet, neither of them taking the time to figure out why this worked. Or why they needed it.

Jade had read enough of Hope's dirty books to understand her feelings weren't wrong. Hell, they weren't even particularly unique. She'd never be a vanilla girl, though in the past, she'd settled for that flavor because it was simpler than offering her trust.

"Do it," she whispered.

Liam gave her a crooked grin, so friendly and familiar, she couldn't stop herself from returning it. "You've been standing right in front of me every day for eight years."

She understood his sentiment, his amazement. "People don't wear their sexual proclivities around on their sleeves."

He chuckled. "It would make life a hell of a lot easier if they did."

She laughed. "Maybe we should propose it at the

next city council meeting. Bet Bucky's a toe sucker. That bastard is always making comments about my feet."

Liam shook his head, his smile growing. "Twenty bucks says Martha Suire is into pony play."

"Your sleeve would say Dom who likes to spank women and pretend he's in charge."

"And yours would say very bad closet sub who's into pain."

Jade sobered up, glancing at the crop. "I want to feel it."

"Why?"

She bit her lip. "I don't know."

"Yes, you do. Say it."

The words fell from her lips without thought. "I'm tired."

Liam raised his arm, swinging the crop. He hit the fleshiest part of her ass with only a small bit of force. There was a brief instant of stinging that mellowed out quickly, turning to heat. "Of what?"

The crop lay still by his side as he awaited an answer. Jade hated the questions. She wanted to give him her body. Why wasn't that enough for him?

"I'm tired of trying to control everything."

Liam lifted the crop again, this time the leather caught her on her upper thigh and the pain lasted longer, burned hotter.

"Like what?"

Damn him. She didn't want this. Didn't feel the need to bare her soul to him. This was just sex. Why couldn't he understand that and leave it alone?

He didn't move, didn't give her more of the pain she craved.

"I don't know, okay? Just everything. Of feeling so helpless, of watching Vivi slip further and further away and not being able to do anything to stop it. Of trying to be two kids instead of one, of feeling guilty for living when George didn't…" Her words became trapped in the lump in her throat. She shook her head, trying to warn him off, to shake out all the shitty feelings clambering down on her. She swallowed hard, refused to cry. Finally, she found her voice once more. "I'm just tired, Liam."

    Liam didn't reply. Instead, he gave her what she longed for. He struck her a half dozen glorious times more with the wicked crop, varying the placement, the intensity. Jade's body ignited, burned. She nearly lost her balance twice. Both times, Liam was there to steady her, to support her.

    Tears streamed down her face—of pain, relief, arousal.

    Then Liam tossed it down and stepped in front of her. With one arm wrapped around her waist, he touched her sex with his free hand. His strokes were firm, sure, perfect.

    She trembled, crying out loudly as she came, just before Liam released her arms, there to catch her when she fell forward. For several moments, neither of them moved nor spoke. Jade soaked up his strength, let it bolster her, replenish her.

    He placed a soft kiss against her brow, whispering, "You don't have to do any of this on your own anymore. I'm here."

    His soft assurance triggered something inside her. Opened a door she'd thought locked forever. She slid along his body, dropping to her knees. Unfastening his jeans, she relished the sound of his sharp inhalation as she freed his cock.

    Jade took him in her mouth, encapsulating the head, sucking deeply. Liam clasped her cheeks in his hands, her name sounding almost reverent as he whispered it, once, twice, then again.

She wrapped her hand around the base of his dick, squeezing it firmly as she took more of him into her mouth. He shared her love of rough touches. Recalling that, she pulled back until only the head remained, then she nipped at the tip of his cock.

He groaned and his hands tightened on her face. She felt adored when he held her like this. Jade had never wanted this connection during sex, never craved emotional bonds. For her, sex was an end to a means. When she was horny, she found a way to appease herself—either with a lover or by her own hand.

Caring, friendship and comfort had never figured into the equation. Now she wondered how she had ever enjoyed the act without them.

She sucked Liam deeper, taking him as far as she could, swallowing the head of his cock. He caressed her hair, telling her without words exactly what she was doing to him.

Jade gave herself over to the moment, taking his cock quicker, deeper. She touched his balls, stroked his thigh, hummed her assent when his fingers tangled in her hair, tugging lightly.

Liam had given her so much. So much more than she had offered in return. When she stacked the piles side by side, there was no competition. He'd held nothing back, sharing so much of himself while she constantly kept her distance, leaving huge parts hidden, tucked away, protected.

She didn't do that this time. Today she'd let it all go. He'd helped her do that. Now it was his turn.

She tightened her grip on his cock, swallowed his head once more, dragged her teeth and tongue along all the sensitive parts she'd found during her explorations.

"God, Jade. I can't hold on."

It was all she needed to hear. She doubled her efforts, sucking harder, deeper, faster, thrilled when

Liam's body shuddered, his large frame trembling with the force of his climax.

Spurts of come filled her mouth and she swallowed them down. Then she released him. Liam dropped to his knees in front of her, kissing her deeply, telling her with actions rather than words how much he loved her.

She jerked back.

Liam frowned, confused by her abrupt action. "Jade?"

She knew his face, read his expressions, understood this man. Jade forced herself to look into his eyes. And there it was.

Love.

No one had ever looked at her with that emotion, but it didn't matter. Jade recognized it just the same.

She licked lips that had suddenly gone dry. "We should get dressed in case someone comes in."

Liam tilted his head, clearly annoyed by her desire to cut the interlude short. "No one's coming."

"Even so." She stood, walking away from him, back to where she'd left her clothing in the middle of the barn. Her hands were shaking and tears streamed down her face. She fought like hell to stem the flow.

Before she could get dressed, Liam was there, enfolding her up in his strong embrace. "Take a minute, Jade. Settle down."

She accepted his hug, wrapped her arms around his waist and clung to him. Time passed slowly as she let his soft swaying and quiet *shh*'s comfort her. He didn't try to talk, didn't ask her any questions she couldn't answer.

Instead, he just held her. Let her be until she got her bearings, caught her breath, found a way to stand on her own two feet again. It was always that way with Liam. When she lost her way, he found her, brought her home.

Finally, when she felt capable of facing her life once more, she took a step back and started putting her clothing back on. "It's getting late. I need to get a shower before heading to Spurs. Bruce finally took my advice and hired some extra help. Trevor Jenkins is starting tonight and he's sticking around until close, so you don't have to come in. I'll get him to walk me to my car."

"Is this you running away?"

She frowned. "No. I'm going to work. There's a difference."

Liam zipped up his pants but left the button undone. Jade wished she didn't find that look so hot.

He pulled her face close to his. "We got a little too close to the fire."

She shook her head. "I have no idea what you're talking about."

"Yes, you do. But I'm letting you off the hook anyway. You aren't the only one who needs some time to think, to get their head on straight."

It was the only thing he could have said to calm her down. To soothe the ragged parts of her that couldn't quite understand what had just happened. Throughout everything, Liam had seemed so sure of what they were doing, of what he wanted. The idea that he was rattled as well comforted her.

"Just so you know—the fling's not over, kiddo."

She raised one eyebrow, hoping the look hid exactly how much she'd been freaking out. "I don't remember saying it was."

Liam gave her a quick, hard kiss. "We have until the end of August to figure it all out."

In the past, she would have run out of this barn as fast as her feet would carry her. But Liam had sparked something inside her. She wanted to explore it. He'd just admitted that the time limit stood, the boundaries that protected her were still in place. It gave her the courage to return. "I'm not bowing out, cowboy."

His thumbs stroked her cheeks in that way that she loved way too much.

"I have to go."

"I know." He dropped his hands, allowing her to take a couple steps back. The distance didn't help. He still overwhelmed her, consumed too much of her space. "I'll be at Spurs around ten."

She didn't even bother to argue with him. If Liam said he would be there, he would, and it didn't matter a lick what she said. She didn't even bother to chastise herself for how happy she would be to see him. "Fine."

Chapter Nine

Jade wiped the sweat from her brow, then put her hat back on to shield her eyes from the hot sun. It was mid-August and there wasn't a speck of hope for cooler weather anywhere on the horizon. The summer had been a bitch, beating down on Wyoming for nearly two months without providing a drop of rain. In addition to the normal ranch chores, Jade had spent a fair amount of time hauling water to the cattle as the streams had run dry.

She leaned against the fence, watching a couple hands help Liam with Fearless. They'd put a rider on him for the first time last week and the bull had lived up to their expectations. Hell, Fearless had surpassed them. He was one mean-ass bull. She grinned as the bull kicked out against the training straps with enough force to nearly drag all three men off their feet.

Jade could just imagine the line of rodeo cowboys lining up in hopes of going eight seconds on him. Good luck with that. Her uncle Seth had told her about Bodacious, the world's most dangerous bull. Like Bodacious, Fearless had a dangerous kick that would no doubt buck off even the most seasoned riders. While Liam didn't say as much, she knew he was excited by Fearless's prospects. Owning such a bull would not only be profitable, it would build upon Circle H's reputation, make them a real competitor in the business of outfitting rodeos.

Jade hoped all of that came to pass. No one worked harder or deserved to see genuine success more than Liam.

Liam handed a strap over to a third ranch hand before walking to where Jade stood. "I'm going to have to run into town. I'm meeting Jesse Wilkins and his son about providing some broncs for the amateur competition they're organizing next month. Want to ride along?"

Jade shook her head. "Nope. Jesse's son is a pervert. Not interested in spending an hour with the asshole staring at my tits and making suggestive comments under his breath the whole time."

Liam wrapped his arm around her shoulder, tugging her closer. "Didn't realize that's what classified someone as depraved in your world. So I guess I'm one too?"

She laughed. "Oh yeah. You're a huge perv."

Liam kissed the top of her head. "I love you, kiddo. I'll see you this afternoon."

He pulled his truck keys out of his front jeans pocket and got in the pickup without ever realizing the wake he left in his departure.

She watched him pull away, panic rearing its ugly head. For two months, they'd worked, eaten and slept side by side, but never once had they spoken the word *love* aloud. Because of that, Jade had let herself pretend it didn't figure into the equation.

Jade looked around Circle H, seeing the house, the barn and the pastures through different eyes. She'd come to consider this place her home.

And she was in love with Liam.

"Fuck," she whispered. She'd done it. Let him get

too close. Her heart began to race—with fear, panic. Jade tried to calm her breathing, but it was pointless. Frantically, she glanced around the ranch, searching for an answer.

A way out.

Her gaze landed on Angel, the bucking bronc Liam had recently purchased. It was an amazing horse—strong, tough, perfect.

"Hey, Bucky. Give me a hand, will you?"

Bucky walked over, frowning. "Hand with what?"

"I want to put a saddle on Angel."

"What the hell for?"

Jade looked skyward, praying for patience, her nerves tattered. If Bucky tried to talk her out of what she planned to do, she'd punch his lights out. "Because I'm going to ride him."

Bucky shook his head. "Are you crazy?"

Jade narrowed her eyes, her hands on her hips. "No. I'm not. I break horses on Compass Ranch all the time. This isn't that much different. Now are you going to help me or am I going to tell your sister about you sleeping with those two buckle bunnies in her bed when she was away for that religious revival last month?"

Bucky took off his hat and beat it against his jeans. "Now come on, Jade. Let's don't get mean about it. Judy would skin me alive if she knew about that. She already thinks I'm going to Hell, praying for my damn soul day and night. I don't need her sending me there any earlier. Why don't we just wait until Liam gets back? Make sure he's okay with this."

Jade's temper erupted. "I don't need Liam Harrison's permission to do a fucking thing."

"Well, dammit, I do. He wouldn't like this."

"Isn't it a shame I don't live my life to make sure Liam's happy?"

"That horse is too new, Jade. We don't know what he's capable of yet. What about Jewel? She'll give you a good spin. Lots of kick in her."

"No. I want Angel."

Bucky muttered a slew of choice words under his breath, but then, finally, he grabbed a saddle, getting the horse ready for Jade.

"Damn suicide," Bucky said as she climbed the fence, ready to mount.

Jade was offended by his lack of confidence in her. Angel wasn't the first wild horse she'd ever ridden and he wouldn't be the last. She loved the thrill of holding on—woman versus beast. "I'm not *that* bad a rider."

"Not talking about you. When Liam finds out I put you on this horse, he'll break my neck."

Jade rolled her eyes. "You ready?"

Bucky nodded grudgingly, then opened the gate to set Angel loose. Jade tightened her grip, grinning at the strength of the horse's first powerful leap. For several seconds she lost all sense of her surroundings as the battle between her and the horse raged.

However, her concentration broke when she heard someone yelling her name. She turned just in time to see Liam scaling the fence. Her grip slipped as Angel gave one last, powerful buck.

Jade flew through the air, dust and dirt clogging her lungs and blinding her as she fell to the dry, brown ground.

She landed hard, the wind knocked from her, but she didn't have time to consider that before she was dragged up and pulled out of the corral.

She grasped her head in an attempt to stop her brain from rattling around. Once the world stopped moving, she heard Liam's voice.

"What the fuck were you doing?"

"Riding Angel."

Her short answer seemed to give Liam an apoplexy as he threw his hands in the air, leaning over her, pure fury radiating from him.

"Do you have some sort of death wish?"

"No. I don't."

Liam squeezed her upper arm tighter as he dragged her across the yard. "Oh yeah. That was obvious from the fact you were sitting on your ass with that horse's hooves just inches from kicking you in the head. Jesus, Jade!"

"I wouldn't have been on the ground if you hadn't distracted me. Did you see how long I stayed on?"

Liam's face flushed a brighter shade of red. Jade wondered if she'd ever seen him so angry. "Bucky!"

"Yeah, boss?" Bucky jogged up next to them, clearly afraid he'd be fired for his part in Jade's stupidity as Liam continued to drag her toward the house.

"Call Jesse. Tell him I can't make it."

"Sure thing."

Liam stopped and turned to look at the ranch hand. "And I'll deal with you after I've taken care of Jade."

Bucky bowed his head, guilt and anxiety at war in his expression.

"It wasn't Bucky's fault. I coerced him."

Bucky shot her a grateful look, but her defense didn't appear to help much.

"Don't give a shit. He got you up on that horse. I'm not likely going to forget that anytime soon."

Jade tried to shake off Liam's hand, but his grip was implacable. "What are you doing here anyway? What about the meeting?"

"I forgot the contracts. They're on the kitchen

table."

"Oh."

"Did you really think you were going to take a joyride on one of my best horses without me finding out?"

Actually, she knew he'd find out. While Bucky wouldn't have said anything, the other hands would have filled Liam in the second he got home, anxious to share the gossip. She'd expected his anger. It was what she'd been banking on.

Once they were in Liam's bedroom, he released her.

She whirled on him. "Finished with the bully act?"

"Don't test me, Jade."

Jade lowered her head, struggled to take a deep breath, but her lungs had seized, gone tight. The walls of the room closed in on her. She'd ridden the horse with the sole purpose of starting this fight. Now…now she didn't know what to do. "I need to leave."

"Why?"

"I just need some space, okay? You're suffocating me."

Silence fell as Jade fought to find some semblance of composure. Liam walked to the bed and sank down on the mattress. "What happened? What freaked you out?"

"You're changing the rules again."

He frowned. "How?"

"Is this a fling, Liam?"

He didn't respond, his silence answering her question.

"It was never that to you, was it?"

He looked at her, but again, silence was her response.

"I can't be what you need. I'll never be the meek,

quiet little woman who doesn't blink twice without permission. I can't be *her*. I'll never be her."

"Who?"

"Celia."

Liam reared back as if she'd punched him. "I don't want a Celia replacement. I want *you*."

"Why?"

"You don't get it, do you, Jade? You don't see it."

Suddenly she felt exhausted, worn out. She wanted to go home to her little cabin on Compass Ranch, crawl into her bed and sleep for the next five or six years. "You lied to me. This whole summer has been one big fib."

Liam didn't bother to deny it. "Yeah. It was. I didn't go into this thinking it would end with Sienna and Daniel's wedding."

"What were you hoping for?"

"Something a lot more long-term."

"You said you loved me."

He sighed, nodding as understanding lit his face. "Got it. Now I see. So you got up on the horse to piss me off. To pick a fight."

Jade looked down at her hands. "I told you I suck at relationships."

Liam chuckled, though the sound was more sad than amused. "You're right. You do." Liam stood and walked toward her. Then he cupped her face and forced her to look at him. "But I still love you."

He tugged her closer, kissed her softly. Soon his touches became more passionate.

Jade tried to take a step away, but he wouldn't release her. "Sex isn't going to change how I feel, Liam."

"I know that. But right now, it's all I have to offer that you'll accept." He continued to kiss her, his lips worshipping her mouth, cheeks, ears, neck. He burned a sensual path along her skin until Jade stopped caring about the lies, the future. All of it.

She wanted him.

Jade tugged his T-shirt over his head, doing a little lip reconnaissance of her own. She kissed his chest, licked his tight brown nipples, bit his pecs. Words faded, giving way to actions.

In this, they were connected, similar. Liam undressed her. As he worked to remove her clothes, her hands were busy stripping him as well. Within minutes, they were naked and they fell onto the bed, their limbs tangled together as they kissed, touched, caressed, stroked.

Jade ran her fingernails along his back when Liam took her under him. His lips never left hers as he placed his cock at her opening and pushed in. He thrust hard, deep, sure. The rhythm was familiar, comforting.

She wrapped her legs around his waist, urging him to move faster. Through it all, their lips were connected. Jade loved sharing the same air, savored his smell, his taste. In just two short months, Liam had enmeshed himself in every part of her world— claiming her work hours, her meal times, holding her as she slept. Now she couldn't imagine doing any of those things without him.

His fingers grazed her clit, drawing her back into the moment, away from the thoughts that left her unsettled.

"This is as easy as breathing, Jade. Just let go."

She knew he wasn't talking about sex, but it was simpler to pretend he was. Her body trembled as she let the climax claim her, wash away every worry, every fear.

Liam joined her, his body tensing as he came. For several minutes, neither of them moved, made no attempt to part.

Jade was the first to pull away. She started to rise, but Liam refused to let her go. Tugging back the sheets, he tucked her beneath them with him.

"Stay here," he whispered. "Just a little longer."

She allowed herself to accept the embrace, to soak up the closeness, the intimacy. Closing her eyes, Jade gave in to the fatigue of the past few weeks, letting sleep claim her in a rare afternoon nap.

"What are you doing here?"

Jade dropped her suitcase by the door, then walked over to sit down on the couch, exhausted, frustrated. "I live here."

Sterling claimed the spot next to her. "Oh jeez. What did you do?"

"Why do you assume I'm the one who screwed things up?"

Sterling grinned at her. "Didn't you?"

Jade narrowed her eyes, gave her cousin a dirty look. "Yeah. But you could at least pretend I'm not always a fuckup."

"Sorry. So let's have it. What happened?"

"He turned all possessive and controlling on me. Started trying to tell me what I could and couldn't do. I don't play that way."

Sterling frowned. "That doesn't sound like Liam. What did he tell you not to do?"

"I hopped on the back of one of his bucking broncs. Felt like taking a ride. He freaked out about it."

"No shit. I mean, did he say it was okay…before you did it?"

Jade shook her head, trying to ward off the headache looming.

"Jesus. Why would you do something so stupid?"

Jade rubbed her eyes wearily. She was tired of

lying. To her cousin, to Liam, to herself. "He said he loved me."

Sterling leaned her head back and looked at the ceiling, disappointment rife on her face. "Ah. He committed the cardinal sin. Now I'm starting to get the picture. So you reverted to character and found a way to sabotage the relationship."

"I don't ruin my relationships."

Sterling stood up, throwing her hands into the air with frustration. "Dammit, Jade! That's all you ever do. It's been the same pattern since high school."

Jade was too shattered to argue. Besides, she couldn't find the words to defend herself. She'd gotten on that horse because she'd known it would infuriate Liam. She'd wanted to provoke the fight because it would give her a chance to get away.

Unfortunately, Liam wasn't fooled. He'd dragged her to his bedroom and made love to her. Her stomach clenched.

Why did a word that usually gave a person so much joy scare the shit out of her? It was always the same. Someone would get too close and she'd take off in the opposite direction as fast as her Harley would carry her.

Liam had rolled over when she left his bed less than an hour ago, watching in silence as she packed her things. Once the suitcase was filled, she'd sat down on the edge of the mattress.

"So that's it?" he'd asked.

"I just need some time to figure stuff out."

Liam had given her a sad smile. "Looks to me like you already have."

She'd wanted to protest, but he'd sat up and placed a soft finger against her lips. "Do what you have to do, kiddo."

He'd kissed her, then said goodbye.

She'd driven straight here, fighting like the devil to hold in the tears. She didn't bother to pretend that she wouldn't shed a lot of them tonight.

Sterling plopped down on the chair across the room. "Do you remember Sienna's sixteenth birthday?"

Jade nodded, confused by Sterling's sudden change of subject. "Sure. We had that sleepover." They'd snuck up to the hayloft with a bottle of tequila Jade had smuggled out of her dad's liquor cabinet. They'd gotten wasted, then busted by Uncle Seth and Jake. "What does that have to do with anything?"

"You made a vow that night. I didn't think much of it at the time because we were just kids. What the hell did we know about love and relationships? You said you planned to always be the person who did the breaking up. That you'd never let anyone hurt you. Do you remember that?"

Jade would never forget it. They'd been talking about some girl at school whose boyfriend had dumped her. The girl had been devastated, crying for weeks. On its own, Jade suspected Jenna's typical-young girl response wouldn't have made much of a mark on her. But something else happened around the same time and combined, the two events had made a lasting impression.

Three days after watching Jenna fall apart in English class, Jade had gone to Compass Ranch to ride her horse. While she was out that day, she'd taken a different route than usual simply because it was calling for rain and Uncle Silas had told her to be quick, otherwise she'd get drenched.

She skirted the Compton graveyard, surprised to find Vivi sitting in front of Granddaddy JD's headstone. She was crying. In Jade's entire life, she'd never seen her grandmother's tears, never witnessed such heartbroken agony. Jade had sat there for only a few minutes, uncertain if she should stay to comfort her grandmother or if she should leave. She opted for quietly slipping away, realizing Vivi wouldn't want Jade to see her so sad.

Jade had cried herself to sleep that night, promising herself she'd never let anyone into her heart. Never open herself up for such excruciating pain. Then, at Sienna's sleepover, she'd shared that vow with her cousins.

She'd meant the words. And, because she had more than her fair share of Compton stubbornness, she'd managed to remain true to that oath for eight years.

Until Liam came along with his offer of a summer fling.

Now...

Sterling broke the silence that had fallen between them. "Liam is one of the nicest guys I've ever known, Jade. He loves you and he'd never hurt you. I can't understand why you would choose to live alone when something so wonderful is sitting right there in front of you."

Because love doesn't last forever. The words lingered on Jade's lips, but she didn't speak them aloud. Instead, she stood up and grabbed her suitcase.

"It just wouldn't work, Sterling." She started to head to her bedroom, but Sterling wasn't finished making her case.

"This is a shitty way to live your life, Jade."

Jade knew her cousin was right, but she simply wasn't strong enough to face the alternative.

Chapter Ten

Jade strolled through the graveyard, not bothering to turn on the flashlight on her phone. She'd become a regular midnight visitor here since her sixteenth birthday, and the darkness no longer disturbed her. A week had passed since she'd packed her bag and left Liam's house under the guise of "figuring things out".

So far all she'd managed to sort out was her closet, the kitchen cabinets, the space under the bathroom sink and the storeroom at Spurs. She'd been a cleaning maniac, taking on one tedious task after the other because it helped her avoid thinking about anything real.

Liam.

Tonight had been the first time she'd seen him, though she hadn't found the courage to speak to him much beyond a friendly, "Hello. How are you?"

Then she'd plastered on a fake smile, going through the motions of the wedding rehearsal, fighting like the devil to hide her misery because she wouldn't ruin Sienna's big day for all the money in the world. She'd made it through the practice run of the ceremony, the meal, the longest dessert in history and countless toasts to the happy couple.

Finally, the family began to drift away, heading

to their own homes and beds to rest before the wedding tomorrow. Jade had walked to the cabin with Sterling after saying an awkward goodnight to Liam. She'd tossed and turned for nearly an hour before pulling on some clothes and heading here.

When she reached his gravestone, Jade dropped down to her knees and bowed her head miserably. "Hey, George."

The silence that met her greeting didn't usually bother her, but tonight, it merely reinforced how lonely she felt.

"Help me," she whispered. "I don't know what to do."

For several minutes, the solitude of the cemetery remained unbroken, the vast quiet, the darkness offering her no comfort.

Then she heard a twig snap behind her.

She rose quickly, turning to scan the shadows. "Liam?"

Her father stepped onto the path, into the moonlight. "No. It's just me, Jade. I thought I might find you here." She frowned, confused, until her father answered her unspoken question. "Sterling texted me. Said you'd gone out. She's worried about you."

"How did you know where I'd be?"

Dad shrugged. "You always come here when you're sad or something's bothering you. Or—" her father paused, "—when it's your birthday."

"You knew?"

Her dad grinned. "I'm the sheriff of Compton Pass, Jade. I'd be a pretty poor lawman if I didn't hear my daughter breaking out of her room in the middle of the night."

"But you never said anything."

"The first time you snuck out, I followed you, intent on seeing where you were going and then grounding you until you were forty. When you walked here, I decided to hang back. Give you some space."

"You were watching me?"

Her dad looked sad in the moonlight. She tried to imagine how he'd felt knowing his daughter had snuck out of the house to visit her dead brother. "Yeah. Then Liam showed up."

Jade raised one questioning eyebrow. "You left me here with Liam?"

"Dear God, no. You were sixteen. That man was twenty-one years old. I kept an even better eye on you. And I followed you here the next two birthdays too. After that, you and Liam had become friends. I'd gotten to know him. Knew he was trustworthy. That he'd keep you safe for me, so I stopped coming."

Jade wasn't sure how to respond. She turned to look at George's grave.

Her dad cleared his throat, but it still sounded thick, betraying the emotion he was trying to hide. "I know you miss him."

She swallowed heavily, fought not to cry. She'd never mentioned George's name to her father, too afraid of upsetting him.

"I miss him too, Jade. I should have talked to you about this years ago, but I didn't know what to say. I started to tell your mom, but…"

Jade didn't need his explanation. She knew why he'd held his tongue. "It would have made her sad. I'm glad you didn't say anything to her."

Dad rubbed his chin uncomfortably. "I talked to Silas, Seth and Sam about it, but I'm not sure their advice was much help. Hell, we grew up in a houseful of boys. None of us had a clue how to deal with you girls. The teenage years were the worst."

Jade grinned sadly, amused by the idea of her uncles trying to find a solution to something she didn't fully understand herself. "What was their answer?"

Her dad shrugged. "They thought it might be a hormonal, female thing, that it would pass. It didn't, did it?"

She shook her head, unable to hold the anguish at bay. He opened his arms and she fell into them. Let his strong embrace hold her as she sobbed. Cried her heart out for her brother, for Vivi, for Liam.

"I'm n-not g-good, Daddy."

Her father stroked her hair. "What?"

"I always think that George would've been better than me. That he should've been the one to live."

"Jesus, Jade. What the hell are you talking about?" Her father cupped her face, forced her to look at him.

"Look at me. I was a completely average student in high school. I didn't go to college. All I do is tend bar and work on the ranch. Sienna and Hope both went to the university. They help people who are sick. Even Sterling brings people happiness with her jewelry. She's creative. Talented. I can't draw a damn stick figure. I'm just me."

Dad looked confused, upset. "Is that what you've been thinking all these years? Christ. Jade, you're one of the hardest workers I've ever met in my life. I didn't go to college. Joined the Coast Guard out of high school. Sam got all the book smarts, but I figure I've done just as well as him. Even if I'm not a gazillionaire."

Jade chuckled. Her father often teased his twin brother about the fortune Sam had amassed over his lifetime. "I know that. It's just...I think maybe I could have done better. I should have tried harder. What if George had lived and discovered the cure for Alzheimer's or something?"

Her father gripped her face tighter, pure anguish

written on his. "I never want you to say anything like that again. Or even think it. You are your own person. You're not in competition with George and you don't have a damn thing to prove. You're perfect, Jade. My perfect, beautiful, intelligent daughter. I can't imagine a life where you weren't a part of it. So no more of this *what if* bullshit. No more thinking you have to measure up to some lofty line you've drawn in the sky. I only want one thing for you, and that's for you to be happy. Give me that and I'll never ask, never want for another thing."

Her tears began to fall again. Despite that, she tried to smile, fighting to make a joke. "It might be easier if you just asked me to go to college."

"What happened with Liam last week? You've been moping around for days. Given the fact you're here on the eve of Sienna's wedding, I'm thinking it must have been something pretty bad."

She swiped the wetness off her cheeks. "Oh yeah. It was terrible. He told me he loves me."

Dad didn't reply at first, didn't give even the slightest clue to his feelings. Then he released a long, sad sigh. "You ran away from him, didn't you?"

She nodded, a sob escaping.

"Why?"

She laughed sadly. "I just told you. I'm not particularly bright."

"Stop it. You're in love with each other. So tell me the real reason you left."

"I'm scared."

"Of what?"

She sniffled, determined not to cry anymore. "Of everything. Of losing him. Of how he makes me feel. Of disappearing inside him until I forget who I am. He's, I mean, we, when we're together…it's just so intense, so…" Jade blushed, forgetting for a moment that she was talking to her father. There was no way she could explain her relationship, her desires to her dad.

"I understand." Dad averted his eyes, as uncomfortable with the conversation as she was. But something in his face told her he really did comprehend the truth.

"You do?"

"What happens between a couple in the bedroom is a private thing. Something personal. But I think you're a lot like your mother, thank God. She's beautiful, caring, smart. I adore Leah, everything about her. And I'm starting to see the same holds true for Liam and you. That boy would walk through fire for you."

She latched on to the last thing Dad said. "You really think he would? Walk through fire?"

Dad wrapped his arm around her shoulders and tugged her close. Though she wasn't exactly short—she was the tallest of her cousins by at least two inches—she always felt miniature next to her dad. And Liam.

"I think you and Liam are kindred spirits. You've both suffered a profound loss in your lives. It's molded you, shaped you into the people you are today. After all, you found each other in a cemetery, both of you at one of the lowest points in your life. He's helped you grow into the strong, self-confident, independent woman you are today. I'm sure of it. God knows he lets you get away with more than I would. As far as I can tell, he's never really tried to hold you back from something you wanted to do. Instead, he lets you go while hovering close to keep you safe."

"He says no all the time. He won't let me ride Fearless."

Sawyer rolled his eyes. Jade grinned, recognizing the expression as one she used often. "You're not stupid and you don't really want to get on that bull. You just say that to push Liam's buttons. To get a reaction out of him."

Dad was right. About all of it. Liam had spent eight years watching over her, protecting her as she stretched her wings, explored all the things she'd longed to try. However, instead of making her feel better, that realization hurt her even more.

She swiped away a fresh tear. "What am I supposed to do, Dad?"

"Do what you seem to be able to do in every aspect of your life except this one. Be brave. Follow your heart."

She swallowed heavily and looked down at George's grave.

Her father followed her gaze. "You're not living for him, Jade. Let it go."

It was the second time in a week that someone had advised her to let go. First Liam, now her dad.

She took a deep breath and smiled. Dad loved her for who she was and he didn't regret who she wasn't. It was time she accepted that and moved forward.

"Okay. I will."

Sawyer offered her his hand. "Want to spend the night in your old bedroom?"

She nodded. "I'd like that."

"Just so you know, I cut that branch just below your window off. No more sneaking out."

She laughed. "I love you, Dad."

Dad pressed a kiss to the top of her head as they walked along the path that would take them out of the graveyard and back to the sidewalk and home. "I love you too, Jade. So damn much."

Jade tiptoed into her grandmother's room. It was nearly six a.m. and she was beyond tired. She'd spent less than five hours in her old bed, tossing and turning before she gave up and decided to come here. Compass Ranch and her grandmother never failed to comfort her, to set her mind at ease.

Her grandmother had had a pretty good week, remaining alert and lucid for all of the wedding festivities. Unfortunately Jade knew better than to get her hopes up. The good spells never lasted forever.

Though the conversation with her dad last night had helped her, she wondered what Vivi would tell her to do. Her mind was still whirling over everything her father had said, her emotions one big jumbled mess.

Claiming the chair next to where her grandmother lay, she soaked up the scents that reminded her of childhood, of easier times. When she was little, she'd spend the night with her grandma sometimes, crawling into the big bed, loving the feeling of Vivi's soft cotton sheets and the smell of lavender in the air.

"Jade? Is that you?"

She glanced up and realized her grandmother was looking at her. "I'm sorry, Vivi. I didn't mean to wake you. It's early."

Vivi looked at the clock and smiled. "I've spent most of my life living on a ranch. It's safe to say six o'clock is not early. In fact, if JD were here, he'd tease me about sleeping in so late."

Jade smiled sadly. JD was the reason she'd come here. Her face must have given her away when her grandmother reached for her hand.

"What's wrong, Jade?"

Jade bit her lip, trying not to cry. "Everything."

Vivi scooted over on the mattress. "Climb in."

Jade didn't hesitate to claim the spot her grandmother offered, enjoying the warmth it provided. They rolled toward each other, facing each other, and again Jade recalled them lying like this all those years ago.

"I miss our sleepovers." Vivi's comment proved she remembered as well. Thank God. Jade understood that eventually her grandmother would forget her. Jade would have to accept that. In fact, she and her cousins had been preparing for that moment, spending time with Vivi, listening to and then writing down her memories, her stories, so that they'd never truly disappear.

"I do too," Jade admitted.

"You always used to spend the night with me after your birthday parties."

Jade grinned, recalling how she'd drag most of her new toys along with her to this house, playing with her cousins until bedtime. Then, as part of her birthday treat, she would climb into bed with her grandmother and Vivi would tell her stories until she fell asleep. The tradition didn't end until Jade hit her teens and declared she was too old for slumber parties with her grandma. Jade wished she could go back and kick her thirteen-year-old self's ass for being so stupid.

"I'm sorry I stopped coming."

"Everything has its time, Jade. For the first couple of years, when you were just a toddler, I brought you home with me because your mother needed a night to grieve. Those early years were hard for her."

"She missed George."

Vivi nodded. "As the years passed, that pain faded, became more manageable for your mom. But by then, our birthday sleepovers were for me."

"For you?"

Vivi chuckled. "You've always been such a character—all sass and spunk with far too much personality. You make me laugh, Jade. Remind me of the girl I used to be. Many, many lifetimes ago."

Jade was touched, flattered. "You think you and I are the same?"

"I see bits and pieces of myself in all my Compass girls."

Jade squeezed her grandmother's hand gently. Jade wished it didn't feel so bony and frail. In the past couple of years, her grandmother had shed some weight, lost too many pounds for her small frame. Her wrinkled cheeks were slowly caving in and her large pretty blue eyes appeared sunken, tired.

"I wish I were like you, Vivi. You're strong and brave and you always seem to know the right answer."

"Oh, sweetheart. Fact is, when you get to be my age, a great deal of trial and error has gone before. What you think is wisdom is actually me just telling you what won't work because I already tried it and fell flat on my face."

Jade closed her eyes. "I wish things were as easy as they were when I was a kid. I'd lie in this bed and the real world disappeared." She looked at Vivi. "You always told the best stories."

"Everyone has a story to tell, Jade. Maybe I have more than my fair share, but that's just because I'm older than you."

"You've seen so much, lived through so many hard times."

Vivi frowned. "The good has always outweighed the bad. In fact, I suspect if you talked to your parents, you'd understand what you're experiencing right now isn't so different from what they felt when they first fell in love."

Jade wondered how much Vivi knew about what was bothering her, the depression she'd been suffering at the beginning of the summer, her conflicted emotions in regards to Liam. "What do you mean?"

"I was never apprehensive about Sawyer settling down and finding a woman who'd claim his heart because he was always so laidback and jovial, but it wasn't as easy for him as I had expected. He found Leah while he was dealing with grief and anger."

Jade had heard about her parent's romance countless times. They'd been high school friends who reconnected in California several years later. Her mom had accidentally told Dad about JD's cancer, unaware that he didn't know about it. Her dad had said that the year they fell in love had been the best and worst one of his life. "But you worried about the others? Silas, Seth and Sam?"

Vivi nodded. "Silas had more than a few rough years and I was scared he'd work himself into an early grave denying something that couldn't be ignored."

Jade knew about her uncle Silas's time in Alaska. He'd nearly been killed trying to stay away from Lucy and Colby.

Vivi continued, "Then Seth tromped off to Texas, working with those blasted horses he loves so much. Jody soon taught him there was more to life."

"What about Uncle Sam?"

"He was so driven to succeed when he was younger. Determined to move up the corporate ladder. For a few years, he placed making money above everything else. Then he came home, met Cindi, and he learned better."

"Why are you telling me all this, Vivi?"

"Sometimes our destinies aren't always clear, Jade. But we can't let ourselves be blinded by stuff that doesn't matter. Money, society's opinion, success, grief...even guilt and fear. None of those are important when it comes to love."

Jade sucked in a breath as her grandmother added the final two reasons to the list. Vivi knew. She understood. "I'm scared."

"Of what?"

"Of losing him."

"Nothing is forever, Jade."

Jade rolled onto her back and closed her eyes. "Don't you think I know that? God, Vivi, you of all people should understand what I'm afraid of."

"Why? Because JD passed away?"

Jade turned her head, sorry she'd started this conversation. She didn't want to hurt her grandmother. "I can't lose anybody else."

"You're not just talking about George, are you? You're upset about me."

"Don't go to that assisted living community. Stay here with us. Let us take care of you." Jade had ached to say those words for two years, but she'd held them in, chastising herself for being selfish.

Vivi ran her fingers along the side of Jade's face. "Even if I'm living in this house, I won't be around. My mind—"

"I don't care. None of us do. You belong on Compass Ranch. Always."

"This is really bothering you, isn't it?"

Jade nodded. "Not just me." She didn't bother to say how much it killed Uncle Silas every time Vivi showed him a brochure about the place she'd chosen to live out her days or about the shadow that came into Uncle Sam's eyes whenever she tried to talk to him about the money needed to pay for her care when she left.

Her grandmother was determined not to be a burden on her family. So resolute that she'd been blinded by things that didn't matter too.

"We're your family and Compass Ranch is your home."

Vivi didn't reply for several minutes, then at last, she quietly said, "All right."

Jade narrowed her eyes, trying to determine if she'd heard her grandmother correctly. "You'll stay?"

"I never wanted to leave, Jade. I just thought it would be easier for everyone. I can see now I was wrong."

"Can we tell everyone at breakfast that you've decided to stay here?"

Vivi chuckled. "Determined to tie me to this decision?"

"Hell yeah."

Vivi sat up slowly. Jade pushed herself up as well. "We'll break the news together. Tomorrow. I don't want anything to distract from Sienna's wedding. It's her special day. Agreed?"

Jade nodded. "Okay."

"Now I need something from you."

"Anything."

"Stop hiding. You're not a coward, sweetheart, so stop acting like one. I miss JD and I always will. But I wouldn't trade one second of our life together even if I'd known then what I know now. We had a wonderful marriage—full of love and laughter. The best thing I ever did was accept that third proposal of his."

Jade frowned. "He proposed three times?"

Vivi nodded.

"Why?"

"Because I turned him down the first two times."

Jade wasn't sure how to respond, but she didn't need to. Vivi laughed as she added, "I was as stubborn as you when I was younger. The first time JD proposed I was dating Charles. I believe I told you girls about him."

Jade nodded.

"I rejected JD and told him it was in very poor taste to propose marriage to another man's girlfriend. JD just laughed and said he'd be back when I was free. I thought he was the most arrogant man I'd ever met. Can you imagine the temerity?"

Jade shrugged. "Maybe I'd be more offended by it if I didn't know the end of the story."

Her grandmother lightly patted her on the face. "Cheeky little thing. Anyway, Charles and I did indeed break up...for reasons I've explained before."

Jade blushed. "JD asked Charles if he'd be interested in a threesome."

Vivi laughed. "And Charles refused. By then, JD had turned my head and made it hard for me to remember what it was I'd seen in Charles that was so attractive. So we ended things. And sure enough, JD appeared on my doorstep less than a week later, offering the same proposal."

"What was your reason for saying no that time?"

Vivi's eyes took on the same faraway, dreamy look they did whenever she talked about JD. Jade started to understand that even the passage of time— decades—hadn't dimmed her grandmother's love for her cowboy husband. In the past that expression had bothered Jade, made her feel sad for all Vivi had lost. Now she appreciated how beautiful it was.

"Charles had been my first boyfriend and I'd been single less than a week. I told JD I wasn't about to settle for the first yahoo who looked my way. I planned to play the field, live a little. He gave me that same cocky grin and said that was a smart answer."

Jade tugged her knees to her chest, enjoying the story. "What happened then?"

"He returned the next day, offering to take me out for a ride, and I accepted."

"No proposal?"

Vivi shook her head. "No, but he came back nearly every single day for almost two months. We went to the movies, out for picnics, took long rides on horseback. He taught me what a proper kiss felt like...among other things."

"Is this where Landon comes into the story?"

Vivi nodded. "JD encouraged me to experiment, to try new things. The ménage was fun. So was the bondage."

"Vivi! Seriously?"

"Charles had always been a bit of a stick-in-the-mud when it came to the amorous arts—only gave me lots of quick, closed-mouth pecks. JD opened my eyes to a world of long, luxurious, open-mouth kisses that lasted for hours on end. In so many ways, he set me free to truly be myself, to explore my desires. And the things that man could do in the bedroom were scandalously wonderful."

"That sounds so romantic."

"It was. Then, at the end of two months, JD appeared on my doorstep again and when I opened the door, he was on his knee with a ring in his hand. He said, 'Vicky, I love you. I've asked you twice before to marry me and I'll do it again if you turn me down. Put me out of my misery, love, and marry me.'"

"And you said yes?"

Vivi looked at her. "Not right away. I asked him to let me think about it."

"What was holding you back?"

"The same things you're probably worried about right now. That held my boys back when they fell in love. JD was a good bit older than me. What would society think? He was a strong man who needed a wife who could stand beside him as an equal and not lose herself in him. I was young, nowhere near as confident as I am now. And I was afraid of losing him because he had come to mean the world to me."

Jade appreciated that fear. "You felt all that and still said yes?"

Vivi clasped her hand. "Any life worth living needs to be experienced in extremes. You can't have happiness without sadness or love without loss. It's just not possible. Besides, Jade, if you really think about it, you'll realize you're already there."

"What do you mean?"

"How have you felt this past week without Liam?"

"Miserable. It's been the worst seven days of my life." As Jade spoke, the walls came crumbling down. She'd lost him. And she was devastated. "I'm so in love with him, Vivi."

Vivi stroked her hair. "And he didn't even need to propose three times for you to figure it out."

Jade laughed, reaching out to hug her grandmother. "I love you."

"I love you too, darlin'. Now what do you say we get your cousin married off and then we can start throwing a little positive energy toward your future."

"Sounds like a plan."

Chapter Eleven

"You look beautiful." Hope ran her hand along Sienna's veil, straightening the tulle.

Sienna smiled, then took a deep breath, staring at her reflection in the mirror. "I can't quite believe I'm standing here."

Sterling attached the clasp on the bride's necklace, a lovely silver love knot pendant Sterling had designed for Sienna's wedding. "Well, you are. But make sure it's what you want. There's still time for us to smuggle you out of the house if you've changed your mind."

Sienna laughed. "I'm not going anywhere. Daniel's promised me a hell of a honeymoon, and I intend to collect on it."

"Dirty bitch. Figures you'd be more excited about the sex than the ceremony," Sterling teased.

Jade laughed as she listened to her cousins and retrieved the overnight bag where she'd packed all the things she needed to get ready for the ceremony. The four of them had decided they'd get dressed together in Vivi's bedroom. The wedding was set to take place in the backyard, a Compton tradition that had started with JD and Vivi's small ceremony nearly fifty years earlier and continued with all four of the Compass brothers.

Sienna was the first of the third generation to use the beautiful setting for her special day, but Jade knew she wouldn't be the last. The night before she'd overheard Clayton and Wyatt trying to talk Hope into making today's big event a double wedding, but Hope refused, declaring she wasn't about to steal Sienna's spotlight. Even so, Jade wouldn't be surprised if Hope followed in their cousin's footsteps very soon and took her own trip down the makeshift aisle behind the family homestead.

Jade opened her bag and pulled out the bottle she'd lifted from her dad's liquor cabinet early this morning. While they were indulging in tradition, Jade thought she'd start one of her own. She waved the Patrón in the air. "Who's in?"

Sterling's eyes lit up. "You didn't!"

Jade grinned. "I think such an important occasion calls for something special." She'd tucked shot glasses, a shaker of salt and a sliced lime behind Vivi's jewelry box earlier. She grabbed them and carried the whole load to a small table beside the window.

Sienna watched as Jade poured each of them a shot. "I can't get drunk before my wedding, Jade." While her words were a protest, Sienna's face gave away how much she really wanted to participate.

"We're not getting wasted, See. Just taking one small nip so I can propose a toast."

"Well…" Sienna hesitated for only an instant. "If it's just for a toast."

Hope laughed. "We better make it quick. The Mothers will be up here any minute and if they spot that bottle, we'll never get our drink."

Sterling frowned. "I don't think they'd take it away from us."

"I mean they'll drink it all!" Hope clarified.

Jade handed each of them a glass and was about

to lift hers in tribute when Vivi walked in.

"What are you girls doing?"

"Busted," Sterling whispered.

See lowered the glass guiltily. "Jade was going to toast me, Vivi. For my wedding."

"Well, in that case, pass me one of those." Vivi stepped next to Sienna, her hand outstretched.

Jade hesitated. "Vivi. I don't think you're supposed to drink with the medication you're on."

"Good lord, child. Are you trying to kill me? I don't want any tequila. I just want to pretend."

Jade handed her grandmother the empty glass with a giggle. "Here you go."

Vivi looked around at each of them. "You're all so very beautiful."

Jade felt a lump form in her throat. From the expressions on her cousin's faces, she knew they felt the same way she did. For today, they had their loving, wonderful grandmother. If they could freeze time, hold on to this moment for the rest of eternity, Jade had no doubt every single one of them would.

"Can I say something, Jade?" Vivi asked.

Jade nodded. "Of course."

They lifted their glasses. "Here's to my Compass girls. May each of you find happiness, laughter and love."

They licked the salt, drank the tequila and sucked the limes. Then each of them took a turn hugging their beloved grandmother as the tears began to flow.

Vivi swiped at her eyes. "Enough of that. Today is a celebration. Let's not waste it crying. It's time to head down."

They laughed, then Jade followed her grandmother downstairs—wobbling on the high heels she'd donned—her cousins right behind her. She'd break her damn neck before the day was over.

The sound of her mother's music drifted in from the backyard to greet them. Jade loved to listen to Mom play the guitar, to hear her beautiful voice. She smiled, letting the magic of the day, the warmth of the tequila and the sheer joy of being surrounded by everyone she loved envelop her.

For the first time in a long time, Jade felt good. Really, really good.

They walked out a side door, gathering out of sight of the wedding guests, the groom and the best man. Liam would be standing next to Daniel near the rose-laden arch Jade's uncles had constructed for today.

Jade watched as Jody hugged Sienna before taking Seth's arm.

"Let me get your mom to her seat, Sienna, then I'll be right back for you." Seth gave his daughter a quick kiss on the cheek. They walked around the corner of the house together, Aunt Jody already wiping away tears.

"This is it," Sienna whispered.

Jade smiled at the excitement in her cousin's voice, marveled—and even felt a twinge of jealously—at Sienna's complete lack of nervousness. "I'm so happy for you, See."

Sienna smiled at her. "I was worried about you last night. Afraid today would be too hard for you. I know you and Liam broke up."

"I'm fine. Promise."

Her cousin studied her face. "You are?"

Jade paused to consider the question, then she shrugged. "Let's just say I have a goal and with any luck, by the end of the night, everything will be okay."

Sienna sighed. "I wish I was a less selfish person so I could ask you what the hell you're talking about, but I'm excited and having trouble focusing."

Jade laughed. "You're getting married to Daniel.

At this moment in time, that's all that matters."

They took a few steps toward the back corner of the house, halting when Jade muttered, "Shit."

Sterling turned to look at her. "What's wrong?"

"I can't walk in these heels."

Hope frowned. "You were supposed to practice."

Jade tilted her head. "Oh yeah, Hope. Because heels are really practical footwear for tending bar and training rodeo bulls." She tried to take another step, her ankle twisting awkwardly. "Crap." She attempted several more shaky efforts before frustration kicked in. Bending down, she pulled off the size-nine death traps, relieved when she found herself on steady ground once more.

Sienna laughed as Jade rubbed her feet in the soft grass and released a long sigh. "That looks pretty comfortable."

Hope gasped when Sienna toed her shoes off as well. "But…but…we spent days looking for them."

Jade giggled, understanding Hope's dismay. She'd been roped into shopping detail during what they jokingly referred to as Sienna's Bridezilla phase. There had been a month in the spring when Sienna had sort of flipped her lid, insisting that everything for the wedding had to be perfect. Poor Hope had suffered the most, spending close to a week trudging behind Sienna as they scoured every shoe store within a two-hundred-mile radius looking for the perfect pair.

They weren't sure what Daniel had done or said to rein in Sienna's control-freak episode, but they'd bought a fifth of Jack to thank him for it and promised him more if he managed to keep her calm until the wedding. Jade grinned when she recalled the wedding gift she, Hope and Sterling had purchased. It was two open-ended tickets to tour the Jack Daniels distillery in Tennessee. While Sienna wouldn't get the joke, Daniel certainly would.

"Sorry, Hope." Sterling kicked hers off, her eyes closing in bliss. "But damn, that grass is so cool. Feels amazing. Try it."

Hope blew out an exasperated breath but followed suit.

Sienna grasped Hope's and Sterling's hands, who used their free hands to pull Jade into the circle. "My barefoot bridal party. I love you girls so much. Thank you for being my best friends."

The music changed, the strains of the wedding march starting. Seth peeked his head around the corner of the house. "You girls ready?"

They nodded, then formed their line. Sterling would lead, followed by Jade. Hope was serving as Sienna's maid of honor, so she would walk in just before the bride, who was being escorted by Uncle Seth. Jade glanced down, wondering what Liam would think of her in her bridesmaid attire. Her mind raced over the past, and it occurred to her that the only time he'd likely ever seen her in a dress was at Hope's sixteenth birthday party. They hadn't known each other then, so she doubted he even remembered it.

She stepped into the yard, letting her gaze take in the scene. Her family had outdone themselves with the decorations. The entire area was a sea of colorful flowers and pristine white chairs. It was beautiful, but Jade didn't take long to admire it.

Instead, she searched for Liam. She caught only the briefest glimpse of him before the crowd stood and blocked him from her line of sight. Obviously, Sienna had come into view. She kept looking for him as she traversed the aisle, her heart racing when she finally spotted him in his tuxedo.

He'd never looked more handsome. She smiled at him and he returned the gesture, his gaze holding hers as she stepped to the front, then took her place to the side of the altar. She drank in every gorgeous inch of him.

Even as Sienna reached out for Daniel's hand, Jade and Liam didn't break the connection, neither of them able to look away.

She listened as Sienna said her vows, told Daniel all the things he meant to her. It was as if her cousin had peeked into Jade's heart and stolen the words. For the first time in her life, she truly understood what all the fuss about love was.

It was overwhelming, powerful. Amazing.

As she looked at Liam's beloved face, she recalled what her father had said. Understood why Liam was different, special. Unlike other men who had sought to change her, to break her spirit, Liam let her be herself while keeping her safe, protected.

She'd started this summer full of a white-hot anger she feared would consume her in flames.

Liam found a way to tame the fire. He never sought to extinguish it or snuff it out. Instead, he controlled the burn, made it rage in beautiful ways.

Once the I Do's were spoken and the kiss exchanged, Jade's mom began playing once more—the wedding party's cue to walk back down the aisle. Sienna and Daniel led the line as the crowd clapped and cheered. Wyatt stepped forward to usher Hope out, while Clayton claimed Sterling. Liam walked over and offered his arm.

"You ready?"

While she knew he only meant to ask if she was ready to go to the reception, her answer meant something else entirely. "Yeah. Let's do this."

He gave her a funny look, but in typical Liam fashion, he rolled with it, escorting her down the makeshift aisle and toward the large tent where dinner would be served. The Whitacre brothers were set up and playing a slow, country song. They'd likely keep the music soft until after the meal, when they'd speed up the pace and keep everyone on the floor, dancing until the wee hours.

Liam led her to her seat at the head table, then claimed the chair next to her. He'd intended to give her space today, much as he had last night, but something about her demeanor gave him hope. She wasn't avoiding him, wasn't trying to keep as much distance between them as humanly possible. Seeing her last night, watching her try to steer clear of him had hurt. Badly.

He'd left the rehearsal and polished off three stiff bourbons before falling into bed. He'd woken up this morning with a killer headache and a sinking feeling in his stomach that told him Jade was going to give him the brush-off once and for all today.

Then he'd seen her, walking down the aisle in her pretty sky blue dress, her eyes bright, her smile genuine and the pain went away.

"You look incredible."

She smiled at him. "So do you."

"Jade, I—"

"Liam—"

They laughed when they both started talking at the same time.

Liam toyed with the stem of his wineglass. "Let me go first?"

She nodded. "Okay."

"I'm sorry."

She frowned. "Why? I'm the one who left."

"You were right when you said I lied to you. I never intended for this to be a summer fling. I misled you even though I knew how much you wanted to protect our friendship. I've spent the last week going over all the ways I fucked this up. I did everything wrong, Jade."

"No." She shook her head, tried to say more, but Liam continued to explain, needed her to understand how bad he felt.

"I tried to trick you into giving more than you were comfortable with. You were upfront right from the beginning. About all of it. And if friendship is all you're able to offer, then that's what I want. I'll accept that and live with it. Because I can't imagine not having you in my life."

Jade wiped away a tear as she glanced around the room. Folks were milling around, congratulating the bride and groom, looking for their seats at the tables. "Can we go somewhere else for a minute?"

He nodded. They'd serve dinner before introducing the wedding party and kicking off the dancing. Liam steeled himself for the worst as he took her hand and led her away from the tent. Jade prodded him on until they reached the large front porch, leaving the noise of the crowd and the music on the other side of the house.

"You weren't wrong, Liam. I was."

He started to argue, but Jade cut him off. "You offered me everything—your trust, amazing sex…and your heart. I'm the one who should be saying I'm sorry, the one who should be on my knees begging for forgiveness. I was a coward and an idiot, making excuses. I've spent most of my life running from this, from love and happiness. And I don't even know why."

"It's okay." He grasped her hands in his, hard-pressed to stop the smile her words evoked. "I don't want an apology from you, Jade."

She tilted her head. "Well, I don't want one from you either."

Her tone told him she was actually ready to fight him. He laughed. "So I guess it's safe to say the fling is over?"

She nodded. "Yeah. I'd like to drop the time limit, make this relationship a little more permanent. If you're okay with that?"

Liam studied her face, searching for any lingering doubts. What he saw took his breath away. She was finished fighting against this. She was all-in.

"I love you, Liam."

Those words were the greatest gift he'd ever received. "I love you too, Jade Compton."

He bent down and kissed her. After a week without her, thinking he'd lost her for good, Liam struggled to keep it light. He longed to drag her away from the party, to sneak away to his place where he'd keep her in his bed for the next six dozen years or so.

Jade groaned when he pulled away. "Ugh. We have to go back, don't we?"

"I'm afraid so. Come on, kiddo. You and I have never danced together. I like the idea of taking a spin on the floor with you."

"I can't dance."

He lifted her arm and twirled her once. "I'll teach you."

Jade laughed and started to follow him, then tugged on his hand just as they reached the backyard once more. Her eyes betrayed her surprise at how quickly and easily they'd mended the fence. Doubt crept in. "Can I come home?"

He'd never heard a sweeter request in his life. She considered Circle H her home. He nodded. "God, yes."

"Can I quit my job at Compass for good and work with you training the cattle?"

"Absolutely."

Jade gave him a mischievous grin. "Can I buy Spurs?"

He chuckled. "If you want to."

"Can I ride Fearless?"

Liam cupped her face, drawing her nearer. "Never. Not in million years."

She laughed. "Fine. Can I ride you?"

Liam groaned as his cock went from soft to fully erect in record time. "Dammit, Jade. You realize we've still got at least four more hours to endure with your entire family and most of the town. How the hell am I supposed to do that with a hard-on?"

Jade stroked his dick through his trousers. "Revenge is a bitch." Then she walked toward the tent, laughing.

Fearless looked up from the grass he was munching on as she approached. He appraised her with cold, black eyes for only a moment before dismissing her and returning to his breakfast.

She watched him for a few minutes, then took in her surroundings. For years, the house she'd shared with her parents had been her home. Then, after high school, she'd moved to Compass Ranch, making it the place she kicked up her feet after a long night tending bar. Now, somewhere in the past couple of months, Circle H had staked its claim, made her a part of its land. She could see herself spending the rest of her life here. Working with the animals, raising a family, spending night after night in Liam's bed, his arms. Rather than frighten her, the idea felt right.

A roll of thunder sounded in the distance. Jade took in a long, deep breath. The air was definitely cooler than it had been all summer. Rather than dry and humid, it actually smelled damp. Maybe they would see a break in the drought, receive some welcome rain.

She glanced over her shoulder when she heard footsteps behind her.

Liam walked up to her, tucking his hands in his back pockets. "I was a little worried when I woke up in an empty bed. Thought maybe you'd reconsidered."

She shook her head. "I'm finished with second-guessing everything. I meant what I said last night on the porch, Liam. I love you."

He gave her a crooked grin. "I'm not going to get sick of hearing that any time soon. What the hell are you wearing? My T-shirt?"

She nodded. "Yep. We came here straight from the reception. I thought my bridesmaid dress might be a bit too formal for breakfast. Besides, you gave the hands the day off, so it's not like anyone will see me."

"Had to give them the holiday. They were all drunk as skunks last night."

She reached for him, wrapping her arms around his waist. Both of them were floating on a cloud, lost in that wondrous place where the newness of pleasure and lust and love came together in perfect harmony. "How long do you think this feeling will last before life returns to normal?"

Liam laughed. "Knowing you and me? I give it until noon, then we'll likely be snapping at each other over some stupid thing."

She hugged him tightly. "Yeah. You're probably right. So I guess I should do this now while we're still getting along."

She took a step away from Liam, grinning at the confusion on his face when she knelt before him. He glanced around the yard. "Um, Jade. Despite the fact they're probably sleeping off their hangovers, you do realize there are still at least a half dozen hands who could walk by here any second, right?"

She laughed. "God, you're a horny bastard. Not

everything has to do with sex, cowboy."

He tilted his head as she watched the light go on. "I stand corrected. Carry on."

She grasped his hand and kissed it. "I know you've been down this road before, that the concept of getting engaged, of planning to spend a lifetime with someone isn't exactly new to you. And I hope you realize I know what Celia meant to you and I don't want to replace her or make you forget her. She was an important part of your past and she played a big role in making you the man you are today. I'm grateful for that. For her. But I'm hoping that maybe you'll consider marrying me."

A raindrop fell, sliding along her upturned face. He squeezed her hand and started to pull her to her feet. "Jade."

She tugged back, refusing to rise, as more rain fell. "I know I'm a pain in the ass, Liam. I'm loud, abrasive. My laugh borders on downright obnoxious. I have a terrible temper and I'm not exactly good at thinking before I act."

Liam chuckled. "Damn. Why the hell am I with you again?"

She gave him a dirty look for teasing her when she was trying to be serious. The rain started to fall harder. "You done?"

He nodded. "Keep going."

"But despite all those flaws, I'm hoping you'll remember that I love you. You're my best friend. You make me laugh, you make me a better person. I'm stronger with you. And happy. And I want to be able to give you all those things too."

"You do, Jade. All that and more. I love you so much it hurts."

She wiped the rain out of her eyes, grateful for it as it hid her tears.

This time when Liam tried to tug her up, she let him. She wrapped her arms around his neck and kissed him as the sky opened up, washing away all the heat, dust and dirt, offering instead something that was clean and crisp, cool and refreshing.

Jade broke the connection of their lips first. "You didn't let me finish."

Liam wiped a wet strand of hair away from her face. "Say it."

"Will you marry me?"

He nodded. "There's nothing I want to do more."

She laughed as he pushed her against the fence, his lips taking hers roughly, hungrily. They kissed as if their lives depended on it. It was beautiful, sensuous. Then Liam raised the bar, his hands slipping under her drenched T-shirt, discovering her secret.

"Jade."

"Hmmm," she hummed as she ran her lips along his neck, his throat.

"Where are your panties?"

"You ripped them off me last night, remember?"

Liam didn't respond. Instead, he ran his fingers along her sex, stroking her clit until she was gasping for breath. Then he reached for the button of his jeans.

"What about the hands?"

"I figure none of them will be able to pull themselves out of bed until this afternoon. Besides, who's going to go out for a walk in this weather? I want you, Jade."

She slid his zipper down, reaching inside to free his hard cock from the denim. "Prove it," she dared him.

Liam lifted her, using the fence at her back for support as he slid inside her. Jade gasped with pleasure, wrapping her legs around his waist.

His thrusts drove her to the brink quickly.

"Love you," she said as his hands gripped her ass tighter.

The rain continued to fall on them as Liam pressed inside her, filling her body and her heart.

The summer may be ending, but her life was only just beginning.

Epilogue

Sterling propped her feet up on the railing of the small porch of her cabin and watched a bright red leaf fall from the tree in the front yard. Jade had moved out a couple weeks earlier and since then, Sterling had struggled to adjust to life alone. All of her cousins had figured their futures out, found the men who understood them, completed them, made them happy.

Meanwhile, here she sat, watching summer give way to autumn. While the artist in her adored the changing landscape, the bright, vivid colors of the season, she realized she'd spent too much time lately observing and not enough living.

She'd always been able to go with the flow, to follow her heart, but those abilities didn't help her now as she longed for companionship, romance, God…something more than countless hours in a quiet cabin with nothing but her jewelry designs to fill her days.

When she'd complained about her loneliness, Vivi told her love came in its own season, that Sterling would simply have to be patient.

Then Vivi promised Sterling that when she fell in love, she would fall slowly, softly, and it would be beautiful. Sterling had appreciated the sentiment, but right now, she'd settle for going down fast and hard.

Anything.

Another leaf fell. Autumn was here. It was a magical time of year.

She closed her eyes and made a wish. Then she looked around her once more as another leaf fell. It floated on a breeze for several moments before landing gently at her feet.

Magic.

What Happens Next?

If you've enjoyed the Compass Girls so far, don't wait to find out what happens to them next in Falling Softly.

Compass Girls, Book 4
Darkness has crept into Sterling Compton's charmed life, relentlessly stealing what's left of her grandmother's memories. When she happens upon a compelling stranger leaning against a broken-down pickup in the middle of nowhere, grief and a gut-deep attraction spur her to take that too-safe life by the horns.

From the instant Sterling emerges from her Jeep, Viho is drawn to her carefree spirit. Her innocent offer of a ride turns into the ride of his life in his truck bed—and he forgets why he meant to avoid Compton Pass at all costs.

He should have known that karma was waiting to laugh in his face. Especially when Viho figures out Sterling's father is the one who stood between him and the man *he* should have called "father."

Yet it's tough to hate someone who offers him a job. Especially when he and Sterling realize there's a living tie on the way that will bind Viho to her family forever—if he can convince her she's much more to him than an obligation.

Warning: Sometimes it's hard to let go, but every story has an ending. This one has a Native American hero with a chip on his shoulder the size of Wyoming and a vulnerable heroine who has a gift for polishing up diamonds in the rough. Some scenes may tug heartstrings so hard it'll hurt, but the oh-my-god orgasms make up for it.

An Excerpt From Falling Softly:

Sterling barely escaped the laser stare of her cousin, Hope, as she transferred her grandmother to the other young woman's care. Normally they'd sit and chat awhile, enjoying their time with Vivi. Brew some tea, share ranch gossip and cook dinner together so their grandmother didn't attempt to operate the stove without subtle supervision.

Not today.

With her obligation complete, Sterling needed to escape before she ensnared the rest of her family in the turmoil she'd already been exposed to after Dr. Martin's sentencing. Dramatic? Maybe, but that's how it felt.

Rolling the windows down, she let the wind whip her chestnut hair around her face. The tips lashed her and made her eyes water. At least, that was what she identified as the culprit when moisture trickled down her cheeks while she passed through town.

She bounced along in her retro Jeep, letting the rural scenery soothe her. Nature did that for her. It always had.

Blacktop transformed into gravel and tar. Shops became houses and then occasional farms. As the miles ticked by, plowed fields gave way to grasslands. They rolled off to where they met the mountains in the distance. Crystal clear water, which would be freezing if she parked and dipped her toes in, streamed beneath the old wooden bridge she rumbled across. In the distance, a trio of wild mustangs galloped.

Red rocks and scraggly silverberry bushes inspired a design. Finally, the perfect thing to do with those unusual garnets she'd had lying around popped into her mind. She searched the road ahead for a place to pull over so she could haul out her sketchbook to capture the flash of brilliance before it passed.

Except just then, she spotted the glint of sunlight off something distinctly not natural. A hunk of metal. As she crested a gentle hill and neared, she realized it was a busted truck. Way out here, miles from town, it would be irresponsible for her to leave without checking on its most likely stranded owner.

Slowing down, she approached the vehicle. From this distance, it was easy to detect the open hood and the wisps of blue smoke drifting from the engine of the rust bucket. Not a good sign.

But when she got closer still and noticed the man leaning against the clunker, she whistled.

Enormous, he reminded her of a sequoia. Earthy, strong and beautiful. Majestic. One glimpse at him had a thousand ideas sparking to life. Her pencil would be worn to a stub before she could draw them all.

His hair beat hers in both the intensity of its inky blackness and the thickness of its straight length. Classic Native American features made his face bold and strikingly handsome. But his relaxed pose, ankles crossed with arms up and back on either side of him— splayed across the top edge of the truck bed—had her swallowing hard.

Sterling squirmed in the driver's seat.

Despite his seeming casualness, his broad chest puffed outward, making it clear he could take care of himself. Even if she'd been a two-hundred-and-fifty pound rancher in his prime, she'd have been no concern for this guy.

More sharply than she intended, Sterling hit the brakes, stirring up some dust as she bobbled onto the shoulder behind his vehicle. Instinctively, one of her hands flew to her phone, nestled in her wristlet. She peeked at its screen, double-checking the strength of her signal out here. Thank goodness for satellites.

Furiously, she swiped her finger across the device, sending her cousins a quick text. *I found a stray smoking hot man on the side of the road. Going to play the Good Samaritan. Probably give him a ride into town. If I don't text you back in an hour with details, he turned out to be a psychopath, has eaten me alive and is burying the leftovers in the wilderness. Send help. J*

Three beeps pinged off the inside of her vehicle almost immediately.

Be careful! From Hope.

Don't joke! From Sienna.

Hot, you say? Have fun. Jade, of course.

Gotta go. Sterling laughed softly to herself as she tucked her phone away. She'd probably pay for that later—with an epic pillow fight, or having to muck out stalls with Jade, or by baking dessert for the other Compass Girls—but she didn't care at the moment.

Still amused, she glanced up and caught her sexy stranger staring at her. He hadn't moved a single muscle. Not even a twitch. As if afraid of spooking her, he waited for her to approach. His carefully constructed docile illusion didn't fool her for a nanosecond.

Dangerous though he might be, his raw sensuality drew her. She gazed right back at him, noting the rich chocolate of his eyes and the faint scar decorating the corner of his mouth. Cataloging every detail of his flawless imperfection, she clutched the steering wheel with both hands.

He seemed sort of familiar and yet unlike anyone she'd ever known. So much *more*.

She swore she could read a million thoughts in his stare during the span of a single heartbeat. What the hell?

And then he smiled.

It seemed a tiny bit contrived, and not as reassuring as he probably intended. Like a Big Bad Wolf whose grin only showed off his fangs. Yet, it might have been the most gorgeous thing she'd seen in a year.

Considering the gems surrounding her day in and day out, that was saying something.

Her fingers trembled as they opened her door.

When she slid out of the Jeep, her boots weren't as steady on the ground as she would have expected….preferred, really.

It must have been the trip to the hospital throwing her off her game.

Sterling had halved the distance between them, coming to stand with her feet apart and her thumbs hooked in the pockets of her denim skirt, before either of them spoke. She broke the silence. "Truck crapped out on you, huh?"

"Yep." He still didn't budge. As if that might make her less aware of the fact that he could overpower her in a hurry, if he was so inclined.

"Waiting for roadside assistance?" She wondered why he was so calm. Most people, even seasoned ranch hands, would be leery about spending the night so far out of touch from town. Without proper supplies, it wouldn't be very comfortable at best and could be dangerous if the person stranded didn't have at least moderate survival skills. Already the air grew brisk enough that she resisted the temptation to hug herself.

"Nah. Don't have a cell." He shrugged, the motion only highlighting the ripped shoulders beneath his thin T-shirt and the chiseled sinew of his forearms.

Who didn't carry a phone these days? Maybe he couldn't afford one, if his truck and ripped jeans were anything to guess by.

"So you're just going to chill out here and hope

for someone to pass by?" She arched a brow at his nonchalance.

"Seems to be a solid plan so far." This time his grin seemed genuine. "I didn't expect my rescue squad to be quite so pretty, though. Lucky me."

Bright white teeth flashed from behind his smile. It hit her in the gut, knocking the wind from her as if she'd fallen off one of the ranch horses. Full lips curved upward and his eyes danced with reflected light. She'd only seen eyes so vibrant, with flecks of gold, like that on one other person in her life.

He could have been the very definition of *alive*. The something elusive she'd been craving after this afternoon's bleak reminder of her mortality.

Life's irony gripped her, and she laughed. At her acquaintance's wit and flirting, some. But mostly at the pure exhilaration caused by riding the rollercoaster of her existence. Peaks and valleys. Everyone went through them, clinging desperately to the safety rails and trying not to piss their pants on the plunge down, then enjoying the view when things were looking up, she supposed.

Beaming, she planned to make the most of this sudden peak.

Then it was his turn to be rendered speechless. His eyes widened and his pupils dilated as he soaked in her joy and amusement. Fingers gripped the edge of the truck tighter, as if he might give up his charade and finally approach her if he didn't cling to the metal. Maybe even go crazy and shake her hand. Who knew?

Something warned Sterling that if they touched, even with that itty-bit of skin on skin, sparks would fly and risk kindling a blaze that would set the entire early-fall landscape on fire.

So she dodged. She jutted her chin toward the wrench lying abandoned on the tailgate of his truck and the greasy rag beside it. "So I guess you couldn't get her going again, huh? I could take a look. I'm pretty good with machines and stuff like that. Working with my hands."

In fact, her father's best friend, Jake, had helped her rebuild her entire Jeep from junk. The model from late last century suited her perfectly, classic and funky all at once.

"I'm pretty sure it's not fixable." He grimaced. "But you're welcome to poke around if it'll make you feel useful."

"Sure thing. I'm Sterling, by the way." She snatched up the tool and passed within reach of the gentle giant, who smiled softly at her. "If I can't do anything with it either, I'll be glad to give you a ride into town or call a tow truck for you. You know, since you're so scared of me that you can't move, never mind get in my car."

He chuckled, low and half as rusty as his pick-up. When she peeked up at him from beneath his hood, he seemed startled, as if humor hadn't played a big part in his life so far. Maybe it hadn't. He sure looked like a hard man. One she'd love to tame. A challenge the cocky young guns on the ranch and in town didn't pose for her.

Right then she vowed to help him turn around what had to be a shitty day, a perfect match for hers.

When he finally caved and pushed off the truck, ambling to her side, she held her breath. His shadow fell across her, blocking out the sun entirely. Clearly, he'd been slouching. Probably a smart move, though she wasn't the sort of woman to cow easily.

Putting out one hand, he said, "Viho."

"Interesting name." She shook it, marveling at how he swallowed her fingers with heat and a gentle pressure that didn't crush her but didn't treat her like she was delicate filigree either.

"I could say the same." He flashed her another semi-smile. "Mine's Native American. It means Chief."

"Seriously?" Sterling nodded, impressed. "So are you royalty or something?"

He certainly had an air of nobility about him, despite his commoner's clothes.

"Nah." He shook his head a bit. "I guess I could have been. If we still had chiefs, my grandfather would have been it. The small reservation I grew up on looked to him for approval. But getting involved in our government wasn't my path. Causing a rift in our community was never my intention. And besides, I'm nobody's leader."

"How did you know that?" she wondered. After today, she was starting to doubt herself and her life choices where she never had before.

At first, she didn't think he intended to answer. She figured that was a pretty personal thing to ask a guy you'd spoken fewer words to than you'd say to a drive-thru attendant in the course of ordering a meal. But something about him made her feel as if they'd known each other for a hell of a lot longer than three point two seconds. Maybe it was the way he didn't pressure her, letting her take the lead in their interactions and conversation, unlike most guys she met, who were eager to pinpoint anything they had in common.

Some way to get closer to her, either because they were interested in moving up the ranks at Compass Ranch or because they wanted in her pants. Or both. Kill two birds with one cock, so they seemed to think.

Instead, Viho reminded her of Jake, widely recognized as the best man around for taming wild horses. He had that same aloof patience that lured in the wild beasts and made them believe they were safe. And they were. Jake lived up to that implied promise. He cared for all his creatures, went above and beyond to see that they had everything he could give them.

It also could have been the sadness she sensed lurking behind Viho's spectacular eyes that struck a chord.

"First, the place I grew up wasn't the norm. It was culturally conservative. Dominated by a few extremist families that would never have seen past my less-than-pure blood. I'd have spent my entire life outvoted by the rest of the council regardless of how worthy my ideas were of their support. We'd have wasted everyone's time in one giant pissing match, no one moving forward. It's probably cowardly, but getting more involved seemed like a waste of time. Turning that tide was impossible. It never sat right on me anyway. Politics. People shouting over each other instead of understanding the other's point of view. I've always enjoyed being outside, alone, listening to nature…"

No wonder he hadn't been worried about spending the night outdoors.

"What does it tell you?" she asked.

And he shut down as surely as if she'd called him a loser.

"Hey." She paused her examination to lay a hand on his wrist. They both shivered in response. His skin was balmy against hers and his pulse jumped beneath the pads of her fingers at the contact. "I wasn't fucking around. Not making fun of you. I was serious."

"Oh." He sighed. Suddenly he seemed to age, and Sterling realized he was significantly older than she'd first thought. Maybe thirty-five or forty to her twenty-four. A man with some experience didn't sound like such a bad thing to her. Hopefully, she hadn't come off as some punk kid harassing him. "I guess I should have said that when it's quiet around me I can hear myself think. And I don't feel as out of place in the universe. If I stop listening too long, I start to feel like I don't belong here and never have. And that's totally a strange thing to admit. To anyone. But especially to...you know, you."

He scrunched his eyes closed and pinched the bridge of his nose.

"I guess that means we've passed that awkward introductory stage of our relationship." With that lame attempt at a joke, she released him and tried to concentrate. On his words. On the truck. On anything but putting her hands on him again. Maybe sliding her palms beneath his shirt to steal some of his warmth and map the contours of his prime body.

Because suddenly, she really wanted to show him that he was in the exact right place in the cosmos, and so was she.

"It's kind of weird, you know. I've always thought I knew where I was meant to be. But lately, things are changing, and I think that might be worse. Finding out that how you thought things were supposed to be isn't going to last forever, and that your life is your family's, not your own."

"I know *exactly* what you mean, Sterling." He gazed at her with such intensity that she had to clear her throat and deliberately turn away. "And when that anchor gets yanked up and you start to drift, it's easy to get dizzy. To lose your way."

"Is that how you ended up stranded on the side of the road in the middle of nowhere?" She recalled the black, red and white bedroll she'd spotted in the bed of the truck. It looked like he'd used it. A lot. Not just for picturesque camping trips to manicured grounds, either.

"I suppose it was the start of that path." He shrugged, kicking a rock into the distance.

The grief radiating off him reminded her too

much of what she'd been feeling when she left Compass Ranch earlier—the pain she'd been trying to obliterate, if even for a few hours.

So she steered the conversation to less dangerous ground. Like the cooling weather.

Viho rewarded her change of subjects with the hint of a smile and the loosening of his tense shoulders.

As they chitchatted, she tinkered with his engine. It quickly became clear that his assessment was accurate. The thing was toast.

Surrendering, she turned toward Viho at the same instant he leaned in for a closer look. They plastered together. Instinctively, her hands flew to his chest to brace herself. And she smeared grease all over his soft, charcoal cotton shirt.

"Son of a bitch." She tried to wipe a smudge off and only splattered it more. "I'm so sorry."

"No problem." His easygoing nature counterbalanced her impending freak-out, which would only enhance the social awkwardness that had always plagued her. But when he reached down, grabbed the hem of the tee and whipped it over his head, he struck her dumb.

Muscles rippled as he moved, hardness covered with smooth, tan skin she wished she had a right to touch. "Uh…"

"It was an accident. No harm." He wadded up the fabric and tossed it into the back of the truck.

Except there might be some damage to her heart if it didn't start beating again where it'd nearly exploded in her ribcage. It was time for her to admit it. She had never drooled over a man, not even a movie star or that guy she'd exchanged some heated emails with through an online matchmaking site, the way she lusted after Viho. Instant and vicious, attraction seethed between them.

"Sterling," he murmured.

"Yeah?"

"I think we'd better wrap up here so you can take me into town now."

"What if I don't really want to do that anymore?" She couldn't stop herself from being honest when he'd been so open with her earlier.

"Then I'll wait for the next person to come by." He shrugged, but she didn't miss the flash of disappointment in his warm stare.

Did he think so little of himself that he didn't understand her implication?

"Viho, this is not the time to be dense." Brave, sure, she could be. But making the first move in this situation… Well, that was a little outrageous, even for her.

"What's that supposed to mean?" He encroached on her personal space then, and she loved it.

"I think I'd rather stay here with you and listen to what nature is telling *me* right now." She wiped her hand on her skirt, then reached up to his cheek.

"You can't mean that." His eyes went wide. "Are you for real? Maybe I didn't drink enough water today. I've been stuck out here for a while."

Sterling smiled. She knew she was doing the right thing. He'd needed to find her as much as she'd needed to discover him today. For whatever reason, they were here in the same place at the same time.

Wasting that opportunity—divine or pure dumb luck—would not be wise.

Sterling might not have believed in fate before, but she could be converted.

"Does this seem like I mean it?" She launched herself at Viho then, sure he wouldn't allow her to fall. Wrapping her arms around his neck, she went onto her tiptoes.

He didn't leave her straining for long. His broad hands cupped the back of her thighs and lifted her to his level. The tips of her boots dangled off the ground as their bodies aligned. Locking them tighter, she wrapped her legs around his hips and crossed her ankles even as her hands rested on either side of his neck. A breeze cooled her ass when her skirt rode up due to her very unladylike position.

Holding her as if she was as dainty as her cousin, Hope, he stared into her eyes until she lunged forward, plastering her lips on his before he could bring either one of them to their senses.

That was when his gentlemanly exterior sheared away.

About the Authors

Jayne Rylon and Mari Carr met at a writing conference in June 2009 and instantly became arch enemies. Two authors couldn't be more opposite. Mari, when free of her librarian-by-day alter ego, enjoys a drink or two or... more. Jayne, allergic to alcohol, lost huge sections her financial-analyst mind to an epic explosion resulting from Mari gloating about her hatred of math. To top it off, they both had works in progress with similar titles and their heroes shared a name. One of them would have to go.

The battle between them for dominance was a bloody, but short one, when they realized they'd be better off combining their forces for good (or smut). With the ink dry on the peace treaty, they emerged as good friends, who have a remarkable amount in common despite their differences, and their writing partnership has flourished. Except for the time Mari attempted to poison Jayne with a bottle of Patron. Accident or retaliation? You decide.

Join Mari's newsletter and Jayne's Naughty News so you don't miss new releases, contests, or exclusive subscriber-only content.

Look for these titles by Mari Carr

Big Easy
Blank Canvas
Crash Point
Full Position
Rough Draft
Triple Beat
Winner Takes All
Going Too Fast

Boys of Fall:
Free Agent
Red Zone
Wild Card

Compass:
Northern Exposure
Southern Comfort
Eastern Ambitions
Western Ties
Winter's Thaw
Hope Springs
Summer Fling
Falling Softly

Farpoint Creek:
Outback Princess
Outback Cowboy
Outback Master
Outback Lovers

June Girls:
No Recourse
No Regrets

Just Because:
Because of You
Because You Love Me
Because It's True

Lowell High:
Bound by the Past
Covert Affairs
Mad about Meg

Bundles
Cowboy Heat
Sugar and Spice
Madison Girls
Scoundrels

Second Chances:
Fix You
Dare You
Just You
Near You
Reach You
Always You

Sparks in Texas:
Sparks Fly
Waiting for You
Something Sparked
Off Limits
No Other Way
Whiskey Eyes

Trinity Masters:
Elemental Pleasure
Primal Passion
Scorching Desire
Forbidden Legacy
Hidden Devotion
Elegant Seduction
Secret Scandal
Delicate Ties

Wild Irish:
Come Monday
Ruby Tuesday
Waiting for Wednesday
Sweet Thursday
Friday I'm in Love
Saturday Night Special
Any Given Sunday
Wild Irish Christmas
January Girl
February Stars

Individual Titles:
Seducing the Boss
Tequila Truth
Erotic Research
Rough Cut
Happy Hour
Power Play
One Daring Night
Assume the Positions
Slam Dunk

Also by Jayne Rylon

MEN IN BLUE
Hot Cops Save Women In Danger
Night is Darkest
Razor's Edge
Mistress's Master
Spread Your Wings
Wounded Hearts
Bound For You

DIVEMASTERS
Sexy SCUBA Instructors By Day, Doms On A Mega-Yacht By Night
Going Down
Going Deep
Going Hard

POWERTOOLS
Five Guys Who Get It On With Each Other & One Girl. Enough Said?
Kate's Crew
Morgan's Surprise
Kayla's Gift
Devon's Pair
Nailed to the Wall
Hammer it Home

HOT RODS
Powertools Spin Off. Keep up with the Crew plus...

Seven Guys & One Girl. Enough Said?
King Cobra
Mustang Sally
Super Nova
Rebel on the Run
Swinger Style
Barracuda's Heart
Touch of Amber
Long Time Coming

STANDALONE
Menage
4-Ever Theirs
Nice & Naughty
Contemporary
Where There's Smoke
Report For Booty

COMPASS BROTHERS
Modern Western Family Drama Plus Lots Of Steamy Sex
Northern Exposure
Southern Comfort
Eastern Ambitions
Western Ties

COMPASS GIRLS
Daughters Of The Compass Brothers Drive Their Dads Crazy And Fall In Love
Winter's Thaw
Hope Springs
Summer Fling
Falling Softly

PLAY DOCTOR
Naughty Sexual Psychology Experiments

Anyone?
Dream Machine
Healing Touch

RED LIGHT
A Hooker Who Loves Her Job
Complete Red Light Series Boxset
FREE - Through My Window - FREE
Star
Can't Buy Love
Free For All

PICK YOUR PLEASURES
Choose Your Own Adventure Romances!
Pick Your Pleasure
Pick Your Pleasure 2

RACING FOR LOVE
MMF Menages With Race-Car Driver Heroes
Complete Series Boxset
Driven
Shifting Gears

PARANORMALS
Vampires, Witches, And A Man Trapped In A Painting
Paranormal Double Pack Boxset
Picture Perfect
Reborn

format on Audible, Amazon and iTunes.